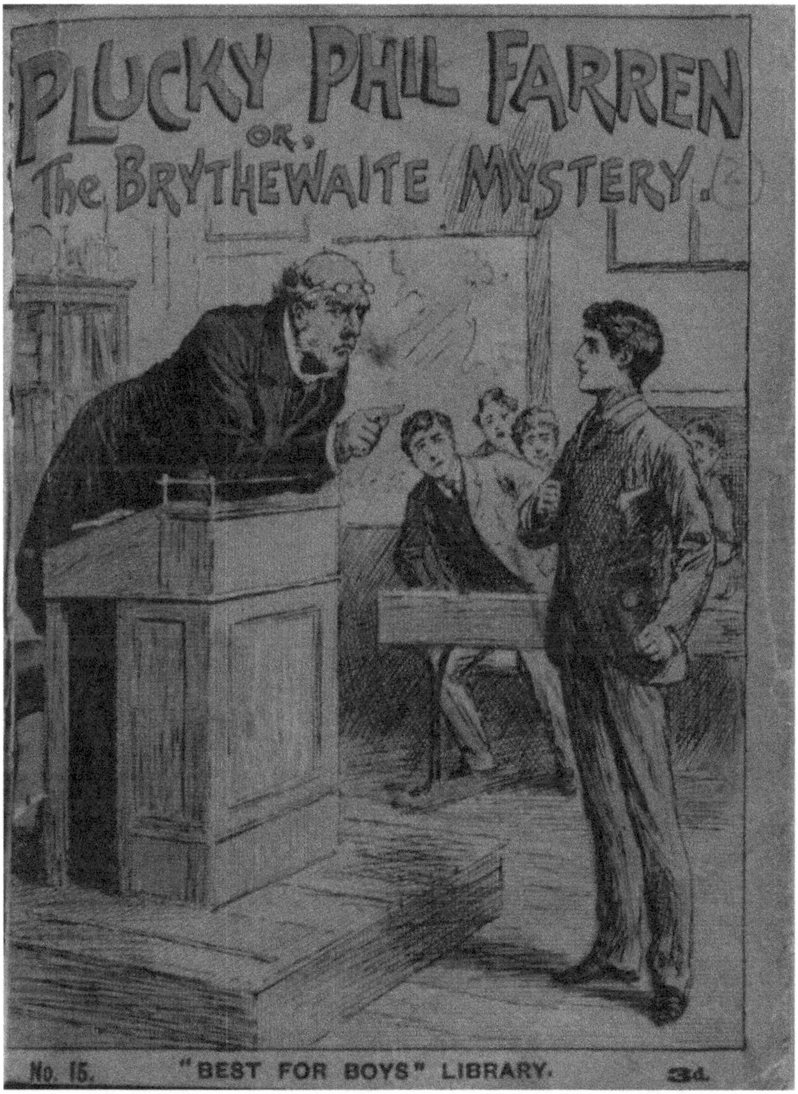
PLUCKY PHIL FARREN
OR,
The BRYTHEWAITE MYSTERY.
No. 15.
"BEST FOR BOYS" LIBRARY.
3d.

PLUCKY
PHIL FARREN;

Or,

The Mystery of Brythewaite School.

—◦◦◦◦◦◦◦◦◦—

By E. H. BURRAGE.

—◦◦◦◦◦◦◦◦◦—

SPLENDIDLY ILLUSTRATED.

PLUCKY PHIL FARREN.

CHAPTER I.

PHIL.

" I WILL now hear the first class in algebra," said Mr. Radnor, the principal of the Brythewaite English and Classical School for Boys, as he opened a book and rose slowly from his seat.

Half-a-dozen of the elder boys came forward and took their places on the form in front of the teacher's desk.

The majority of the pupils looked rather downcast, and the experienced eye of the teacher saw at once that the recitation was likely to be a decided failure.

However, he looked at the class with an expression of encouragement, and singling out the oldest, a tall youth of sixteen, he said, pleasantly—

" Farren, you may commence, if you please."

" I am not prepared, sir."

"Not prepared ?" said Mr. Radnor, kindly. 'What is the matter, then ?"

" Those two problems—the fourth and fifth, sir," answered Farren ; " they were too much for me."

" Don't you think you can manage them if I give you more time ?"

But Farren answered despondently—

" I'm afraid not, sir. I have been working on them all the morning, and I cannot get them to come right."

The schoolmaster seemed vexed, and he was about to make some caustic reply when a thought on another subject flashed upon him.

He lifted the cover of his desk and looked into it for a moment with some perplexity. Then he began to turn over some papers and copy-books.

"It is odd. I am sure I left it here. It was foolish to forget it, and I meant to look for it the first thing this morning."

With a puzzled expression upon his face, he continued to search until he had looked over all the contents of his desk, without finding what he sought.

"It is gone!" he exclaimed. "And yet I am absolutely sure that I left it on the top of these copy-books, where I could put my hand on it in a moment. I do not see what has become of it, unless—"

He checked himself and looked very gravely at the class, and more than gravely at Phil Farren, whose face was flushed. After a moment of silence, he said—

"I did not lock my desk last night. I did not think of it. In fact, I seldom do ; for it has never occurred to me that any boy in the school would open it without my knowledge. I left my purse here and it is gone."

Phil Farren looked his schoolmaster in the face with a countenance which expressed nothing but frank and fearless surprise ; but suddenly the hot colour rushed in a flood to his forehead. The situation seemed to dawn upon him all at once, and he burst out—stammering—

"Oh! Mr. Radnor, I hope—you do not— think—"

He could say no more, but the master, in tones of the gravest perplexity, said—

"Attention !"

At this command the studious boys looked up from their books, and the idle ones pretended to do the same, and all eyes were fixed upon the master.

"Boys," said he, distinctly, "has any one of you been to my desk since the close of school hours yesterday ?"

No one made a reply ; and after a pause he spoke again—

"I left my purse, and it is gone. It could not possibly have disappeared unless the desk had been opened. Does anyone know anything about it ?"

Still no answer.

"If any boy has taken it, I hope he will say so, and not allow another to be suspected," urged the master.

The boys looked around inquiringly at one another, but none of them spoke.

Mr. Radnor searched their faces with penetrating eyes, but saw no look of guilt upon any countenance. Finally he turned to an elder boy, who sat at a desk apart from the rest.

"Morton," he said, "you are monitor this week, and ought to know who was in the school-room after hours yesterday ?"

"Phil Farren, sir. I do not know of anyone else."

"Farren !" exclaimed the master. "Are you sure, Morton ?"

"Yes, sir. I saw him come out."

"What time was it ?" enquired the master.

"Late in the evening," answered the monitor. Nearly nine o'clock, I should think."

Now, it was not an offence to enter the school-room out of the regular hours—it was not prohibited by any rule—but Mr. Radnor preferred that the boys should pass their leisure time elsewhere, and so it was an uncommon circumstance for a boy to be seen coming out of the school-room at nine o'clock in the evening.

Taken in connection with what had passed, it was a circumstance which looked very ill for Phil.

"Farren," said the master, gravely, "this requires an explanation."

But Phil made no answer. He became confused, and blushed and bit his lips in a manner which, it seemed to the master, had very much the appearance of conscious guilt.

"Can you explain how you happened to be in the school-room last night?' repeated Mr. Radnor, urgently.

"I—I—*can* !" faltered Phil.

"You can? Very well ; pray do so."

"I'd rather not, sir."

"What do you mean ?" demanded the master, in astonishment. "Do you not see that your conduct looks very suspicious ?"

Farren was silent for a moment, but suddenly he drew himself up, and lifted his head, with a look half-proud and half-appealing.

"Mr. Radnor," he exclaimed, with quivering lips, and a tremor in his voice, "did I ever tell you a lie ?"

"Never," said the master, promptly, "and therefore I hope and believe that you will be truthful now."

"I will," replied the boy. "And I say, Mr. Radnor, that I never opened your desk in my life,

that I have not seen the purse you speak of,
upon my honour !"

He looked worthy of belief.   He was a handsome
boy ; but it was not altogether his youthful beauty
and brightness that carried the impression of his
truth with such convincing force.

"I cannot think you would say that, Farren,
unless you were speaking the truth," said the
master, seriously.   "I wish to believe you ; and, in
order that I may believe you without a doubt, you
must tell me what you were doing in the school-
room."

"I wish you would not insist upon that, sir," said
Phil, turning red in the face again.

"I must insist," said the master, kindly, but with
decision.

"Well, then," stammered Phil, hanging his head,
but finding it impossible to conceal the laugh which
began to creep around the corners of his mouth—
"well, then, I—I was shutting Martin Blake's
monkey up in the coal-cupboard."

A sudden titter from the class and a broad smile
from the master greeted this statement, which was
instantly accepted as true, for the reason that
nothing was more likely.

Phil was the most inveterate practical joker in the
whole school ; in fact, his love of fun often led him
into acts of reprehensible mischief ; and it was well
understood that when any disturbance was created
n the school-room or dormitories, by some prank or
more than common boldness and audacity, the plot
was pretty sure to have been hatched up between
Phil and his chum, Arthur Castleton.

Any piece of mischief which was not otherwise
accounted for, and which could not very well

be shouldered upon Phil, was generally laid to Jacko. They both had a good share in most of the school scrapes.

But Martin did not laugh with the others. He looked at Phil in blank amazement as Mr. Radnor, who had quickly suppressed his involuntary smile, remarked—

"Why did you do that? To make a disturbance, I suppose?"

"Yes, sir," admitted Phil, with a glimmer of fun in his eyes. "I—thought he'd kick up a row by this time."

"Well, you see he has not kicked up any row; a very sensible animal."

"What on earth are you talking about, Phil?" exclaimed Martin. "The monkey is locked up in his cage, and hasn't been out since yesterday morning."

Mr. Radnor turned sharply around, and a frown darkened his brow.

"What does this mean?" he asked.

"I don't know," murmured Phil.

"How do you know the animal has not been out of its cage, Blake?"

"Because I keep the cage locked whenever I am in my room or here, sir. I've done so ever since the day he got into the school-room in study hours, and you said he must not be allowed to go at liberty any more. I locked him up last night before eight o'clock," said Blake.

"But I went and let him out, Blake, while you were in Henderson's room," said Phil.

"You did?" cried Blake. "Why, when I went to bed he was in the cage, locked up as usual. And he's there now."

Phil looked simply bewildered, and Mr. Radnor walked with angry strides to the coal-cupboard and threw open the door.

No monkey was to be seen, and it was plain to Phil that the master no longer believed the story.

He turned to the lad with a stern, accusing air, and said—

"You see, Phil, that all further attempts to deceive me will be fruitless. Will you tell the truth about this matter?"

"I have told the truth, sir."

"You are clearly convicted of falsehood," said the master, speaking more sternly than before.

Phil grew a little pale, but he looked at the master with steady eyes, and answered—

"If you punish me, sir, it will be undeserved. I believe I never told a lie, much less stole anything, in my life."

"No more!" said the master. "Do not add to your guilt by persisting in it, for it is too plain to be denied. Go to your room, and remain there until this time to-morrow. I hope after twenty-four hours of confinement and reflection, you will come to me in a different state of mind. If not, you must suffer the consequences of such dishonourable conduct."

Pale and silent, but holding his head rather higher than usual, Phil turned and went out of the school-room.

"Morton," said the master, "you will see that Farren is locked in his room, and take charge of the key."

The monitor rose and followed Phil, though with evident reluctance. Outside the school-room door, Phil turned and faced him.

"Morton," said he, in a tone of anxious appeal, "do you believe it?"

"Believe what?" asked Morton, evasively.

"That I am a thief," faltered Phil.

"I—do not like to believe it," said Morton, hesitating.

"But you *do*, though!" and Phil walked on, without another word.

He was bitterly hurt to find that Morton, a youth whose opinion was respected in the school, shared the master's belief in his guilt. Without doubt, he thought, they would all believe it, if Morton did.

But Phil was mistaken, for such was not the case.

When he was shut into his room and left to his own reflections, he thought over what had taken place, and the more he thought of it, the harder it seemed to him that *he* should be accused of stealing.

It would have done him good to hear how stoutly his friends defended him at the hour of intermission, when they were all assembled in the playground.

"There's a mystery in this thing," said John Leslie. "Something is wrong ; but it goes against my grain to believe Phil Farren a thief."

"And I *don't* believe it!" cried Arthur Castleton ; "and you can't make me ! That confounded monkey—"

"Oh! come," interrupted the owner of the unlucky animal, which, with his own spirit of mischief, had got poor Phil into trouble. "Oh! come now, Castleton! You don't pretend to say that the monkey could lock himself up?"

"Somebody else could," retorted Arthur. "Some-

body could have seen what Phil was up to, and I'll
bet a shilling somebody did ! Somebody took Jacko
out of the closet, and locked him up in the cage
again, just to spite Phil. Somebody's got a grudge
against him."

"Nonsense !" exclaimed Morton, the monitor.
"A grudge against Phil Farren !"

And nobody tried to uphold the argument ; it
was too flimsy.

There was absolutely not a boy in the school who
did not thoroughly like the fun-loving, hot-headed,
generous-hearted, mischievous Phil.

There seemed to be very little probability that
Mr. Radnor would alter his opinion.

He was a just man, although sometimes a little
apt to be hasty in his judgment ; but when he had
once made up his mind to any way of thinking, it
required very absolute proof to convince him that
he was mistaken—a valuable quality, in its way,
but not at all pleasant when one happens to be
mistaken.

Arthur Castleton, and others of Phil's especial
chums, went in to their studies with very sober faces
—in fact, an air of unusual gravity pervaded the
whole school. They seemed to be all under the
cloud which hung over their genial and favourite
companion.

At noontide Phil's luncheon was sent up to him
by the monitor, who was requested to ask him if he
had any message for Mr. Radnor.

"What did Farren say ?" the master enquired
when Morton came back and joined the other boys
at the table.

The monitor replied, in a low voice—

"He said, 'Tell Mr. Radnor that I am sorry I did

—not let the monkey alone ; but I have nothing else to be sorry for, except that he thinks I'm a thief and a liar, and I think he will be sorry for that before long.' "

Mr. Radnor looked surprised and displeased, and Morton added—

" He said, 'Tell him that if nothing turns up to clear me, I hope he will try and think as well of me as he can.' "

" Was that all he said ?"

" Yes, sir," answered Morton,

He spoke in a thoughtful manner, but though the master looked at him expectantly, he said no more.

It had crossed his mind for a moment that Phil might have a notion of trying to escape from his confinement and run away ; but he dismissed the idea as unlikely.

It did not seem very probable.   The Brythewaite school-building was an old manor-house, which had been adapted to its present use without much alteration.   It was built upon the banks of a river, close to the brink—so close that some of its old-fashioned balconies and bay-windows projected over the water.

The rooms on the upper story were used as dormitories, and the one which was occupied by Phil Farren and Arthur Castleton was on the water side, and had but one window, an oriel, which over-hung the river.

Morton concluded that there was no chance for Phil to get away, and that he could not have been thinking of such a thing ; and so he did not mention his momentary suspicion.

" There was a mystery somewhere." So John

Leslie had said, and so he repeated more than once during the luncheon hour ; but at a later hour the mystery was cleared up in a very unexpected manner.

CHAPTER II.

JACKO.

As Mr. Radnor was hearing the closing recitation of the day he chanced to lift the cover of his desk, and observed some curious red marks on the edge, very much as if some person had opened the desk with bleeding fingers. It struck him at once that this might be a clue to some evidence in relation to the missing purse.

"Boys," said he, addressing the school, "has any one of you cut his fingers or hands lately ?"

Apparently not, for no one replied, though some of the boys examined their hands, as if to make sure that no casualty of that kind had happened to them unawares.

"I find blood-marks on my desk," said the master, "which looks as if— But stay ! No, it is not blood. I see now ; it is ink—red ink. Who has any red ink ?"

"I had a bottle," said Arthur Castleton, "but I never used it much. Let's see—I forget now what —"Oh ! I put it in the coal-cupboard, up on the shelf. *By George !*"

"Castleton !" exclaimed the master, astonished.

"Beg your pardon, sir !" cried Arthur, in great excitement ; "but I'd like to go and look in the coal-cupboard, if you please !"

"I have no objection," said Mr. Radnor ; "but I do not understand you in the least."

Arthur, however, without offering any explantion, instantly started from his seat and rushed to open the door of the coal-cupboard.

This cupboard, a large one, was called the coal-cupboaid because a quantity of coal was kept there for use in the school-room ; but it was also used as a place of storage for the rubbish of the school, where the boys were accustomed to stow away old books, boxes, and all sorts of odds and ends.

As there was a window in it, a ventilator-window had been placed over the door, allowing the air to circulate through the school-room.

Arthur climbed up on the coal-box to reach a high shelf above, and the next moment he shouted—

"Just as I thought ! Hurrah ! It wasn't Phil ; it was Jacko !"

" What do you mean ?" asked the master, hastily coming to the cupboard-door and looking in.

"Why, don't you see, sir ? Phil did put the monkey in here, and he got up on the shelf and upset the bottle of ink ! There it is, running all down the wall ! And he got into the school-room through the ventilator—it was open all the time. Phil never thought of that. Here's the marks of his paws where he dabbled them in the ink !" cried Arthur, speaking so fast and so excitedly that his words tumbled one over another, in reckless defiance of grammar and elocution.

And having reduced himself to a breathless condition, he made a pause, and pointed out to Mr. Radnor the red marks on the edge of the ventilator, like those he had discovered on his desk ; then jumping down, and pointing to the floor at his master's feet, he exclaimed—

"Here again, sir! See when he dropped down from the ventilator, and left all that ink on the floor! And here—and here it goes right over to your desk, Mr. Radnor!"

There was, in fact, a large red blot in front of the cupboard-door, and little dotted stains of the same colour were visible at intervals across the floor, and quite distinct enough to trace the monkey's supposed progress up to the master's desk.

Arthur was trembling with eager joy, the whole school was excited, and a look of great relief was blended with deepest pain in the expression of the master's face.

He went to his desk and raised the cover again.

"Yes," he said, and his voice was not much steadier than Arthur's own—" yes, you are right, my boy, and I have been mistaken. Thank Heaven, I have been mistaken!"

There was no doubt of Mr. Radnor's profound sincerity in speaking thus, for the tears stood in his eyes as he continued—

"Beyond a doubt, beyond the shadow of a doubt, poor Farren is absolutely innocent. The red ink-marks are here on my copy-book, just where I placed that purse. But what led the monkey to take it?"

"Why, you know he is always imitating everybody, and has quite a love for money," said Arthur.

"And, by George!" he cried, after a moment, bursting out again with his favourite expletive—and for once, the master forgot to reprove or check him — " if Jacko took the purse he's got it yet, for he always hangs on to anything he gets hold of until it's taken away from him. I say, Blake, go and see, will you?"

Blake looked at the master for permission, and, as Mr. Radnor made a quick sign of assent, he hurried away.

In a few minutes he came back, followed by another boy, whose face wore a bewildered look.

This was Henry Lawson, who had been given leave to spend the day with some relatives in an adjacent village and had been absent since early morning.

Blake rushed to the master's desk, and thrust a torn and rumpled purse and some loose cash into his hand.

"There it is, sir!" said he, panting. "And Lawson says—Lawson says—"

My Radnor checked him by a gesture.

"You are out of breath," said he, gently. "What is it, Lawson?"

"Why," said Lawson, in a wondering tone—for Blake had not stopped to give any explanation— "I was just telling Martin that I found Jacko chattering with the door of his cage open in the outhouse before I went up to bed last night. So I just locked up the cage and let him alone. Martin stayed in Henderson's room till the lights were called out, and I was asleep when he came in, and I never thought to tell him of it this morning. Was it anything of consequence?"

"It was indeed," said Mr. Radnor, with a sigh. "Poor Farren! If he was not so fond of mischief, this would not have happened; but I need not have been so hasty in condemning him. I hope this will be a lesson to us both."

He leaned his head upon his hand and sighed again ; and the school was very silent, and the boys glanced at each other very soberly, for they had seldom seen the master so deeply moved.

"Mr. Radnor," said Castleton, softly, "can I go up and tell Phil ?"

"Yes, Arthur, go," replied the master, rising from his seat. "Ask him to come down at once."

Arthur went with flying steps, pausing only to take the key of his and Phil's room from Morton, the monitor ; and Mr. Radnor looked at the clock, and said—

"Boys, it is time to close, but you will please keep your seats for a few moments until Farren comes down. He was accused before you all, and you have all seen the proof that he was accused unjustly. It is proper that my apology to him should be equally public."

This was no more than the boys had expected, for Mr. Radnor taught them, by example as well as precept, to be honourable and manly in their behaviour ; and he had often said to them that when a gentleman found he had wronged another, his duty was to make prompt apology.

Nevertheless, they knew him well enough to be quite sure that Phil Farren would have to translate ten extra lines of Virgil for shutting up the monkey.

But suddenly a sound of clattering feet was heard, and Arthur burst into the school-room, shouting—

"Mr. Radnor, Phil is not there !"

"Not there ?" echoed the master.

"No, sir ; he's gone !"

"Gone ?" repeated the master, again. "But how can he be gone ?"

"*Phil is raving mad! Clean off his head.*"

"Why, I suppose he went through the window, sir, for it's wide open," answered Arthur, coolly. "His things are scattered all around the room, and his—"

Mr. Radnor interrupted him, in a horrified voice—

"The window! It is over the river! Oh! it cannot be that the poor boy has been driven to despair, and—and drowned himself!"

"Oh! good gracious! no, sir!" cried Arthur, quite amazed at such a preposterous idea. "That wouldn't be much like Phil Farren. Why, he's the best swimmer in the school! He has jumped into the river and swam ashore, I suppose, and started for home."

"Ah! then, of course he has gone home," said Mr. Radnor, drawing a long breath of relief. "I will write to him at once, and I hope we shall see him back in a few days."

But it was destined to be many long days before the master of Brythewaite School heard anything more of Phil Farren.

CHAPTER III.

PHIL GOES ON AHEAD.

HAVING made up his mind that he could not remain to endure the humiliation of being accused of a crime which he had not committed, Phil had escaped from his room in the manner described by Arthur Castleton.

Remembering a plan which he had arranged with Arthur and Tom Rich and Will Henderson, he resolved to take advantage of the idea.

Accordingly, he made a bundle of his clothes, his

watch, and his purse, which contained a small remnant of his last allowance of pocket-money, and wrapped them up securely in a water-proof coat which was to have played a part in that proposed exploit—viz., to run away.

He then raised his window, tossed the bundle into the river, and dived after it.

It was only by the merest accident that no one saw him, for the kitchen and all the housekeeper's rooms were on that side of the house, and as it was a warm day in early June, the windows were open ; but no one chanced to be looking out just then, and Master Phil made his leap undetected.

He secured his bundle, swam ashore below the house, and speedily got into his clothes, which were a little wet in spite of the waterproof coat ; but Phil made no account of that.

Being dressed, he started with all haste for Brythewaite village, hoping to catch the three o'clock train for London.

It was true, as Mr. Radnor had supposed, that he set out with the intention of returning home ; but Phil's intentions were not always carried out.

There was many a hard experience of toil and peril in store for him before they saw him in his uncle's house. He was just in time for the train, and was soon on his way to London.

But now his mind began to be troubled with thoughts of his aunt and uncle—how badly they would feel when he came to explain the reason for his sudden return home.

When they heard what had happened, would they credit his side of the story or Mr. Radnor's ? He thought they would believe him, and yet he hated to go home and tell them.

Besides, he would be expelled from the school,
and he could imagine what a blow that would be to
the good uncle who held him as a son, and had all
a father's pride in his fine talents and rapid advance-
ment in his studies; and to the loving aunt—his
second mother—whose tender heart would be
wounded so keenly.

The more he thought of these things the more he
dreaded to go home; and when the train came
into the station, he got off in a most uncomfortable
frame of feeling, and instead of taking the nearest
road to his uncle's house, he walked away, with no
object except to put off as long as possible the
moment when his bad news must be told.

Well, Phil did what many other high-spirited
lads would have done under the circumstances—he
made up his mind to run away to sea.

It was a rash idea, perhaps, but a courageous boy
in trouble is apt to be rash, and Phil went straightway to the docks.

There he met with the usual rebuffs, for no one
seemed to want an inexperienced lad, but at last
good—or ill fortune as it may be—befriended him,
and he came across a captain who was about to
sail, and wanted a smart young fellow as clerk, as
the one who belonged to the ship had just been
taken ill.

Phil's offer to work his way to Natal for his
board was accepted, and before another day had
dawned he was wafted away from home and friends,
far over the sea.

He performed his duties diligently, and met with
no extraordinary adventure on the voyage.

A storm or two was encountered on the way, and
that was all.

In due time he reached Natal, and resisting an offer to ship back, he stepped ashore.

Like the young tiger who had tasted blood he longed for more. The spirit and desires of the traveller had laid hold of him.

Loitering aimlessly about the streets, his attention was attracted to a number of men who were collected in front of an office, apparently interested in the announcements printed on a poster, which hung beside the door—

"HO! FOR THE DARK HILLS,

EXTRAORDINARY CHANCE!

Best Route! Cheapest Rates! Quickest Time!"

These were the conspicuous head-lines which caught Phil's eye as he turned an indifferent glance in that direction.

At that time a gold excitement about the Dark Hills was at its height, and the very name had such an alluring sound that the boy stopped at once and read the whole poster, which set forth that a party was being formed to go to the Dark Hills immediately, with advantages of reduced rates of fare, &c.

A through ticket was to be had for five pounds, and the time of departure was set for that very night.

As his eye took in all this, a wild thought rushed into Phil's mind.

Why should he not be a miner? He would go to the Dark Hills! He would leave all this miserable business behind, and would not come back until he was man grown and had made his fortune by gold hunting.

At least, he would stay away three years, or perhaps five, and by that time they would all have found out that he was not to blame.

CHAPTER IV.

PHIL GOES AFTER GOLD.

IN his usual impulsive fashion Phil rushed into the enterprise without stopping to think about it.

He had no money, but that recollection only served to suggest a means of obtaining the requisite sum.

His watch and chain were very handsome and valuable—a gift from his uncle on his last birthday.

He felt sure that he could sell them for enough to pay the expenses of the journey and buy the necessary outfit; and though he had taken great pride in wearing such a costly watch, and hated to part with it, yet he was determined to go, and he did not hesitate.

In about twenty minutes Phil's beautiful watch and chain were in the show-case of a dealer in second-hand jewellery, to whom he had sold them for less than half their value, and he was returning in haste to the agent's office where that seductive poster hung, with all its brilliant offers of the "cheapest and quickest" transportation to the new "El Dorado."

Almost before he knew it, he found himself in the office, inquiring of a man who sat at a desk behind a railing at what time the expedition was to start.

"Half-past six this evening," was the answer. And it was already past five.

There was little time, but he had no preparations

t make. He asked a few questions about the route, and so forth, and then tendered the price of a ticket.

"For yourself?" said the agent, with a stare.

Phil nodded assent.

"But what on earth do you want with a ticket to the Dark Hills?" asked the agent, still staring hard at the slim, bright-faced lad, with the honest, blue eyes and the brown-gold hair.

"I do want to go, of course," answered Phil.

"Oh, you do! And what are you going to do when you get there?

"Why, work! Hunt for gold—do what anybody does!" said Phil rather vaguely, but with great determination.

"You?" laughed the agent. "You go prospecting for gold in the Hills? Boy, you don't know what you are talking about! Why, it is hard work for a man, and the roughest kind of a life."

"I suppose so ; but I'm not afraid of hard work, and I dare say I can rough it as well as any one," rejoined Phil, with some resentment.

The agent laughed again, in a good-natured way. He had a boy of his own, who had been smitten with the Dark Hills "craze," and he thought he understood Phil's case.

"I see what's the matter with you, my lad," said he. "You want to run away from your home and your friends, and go out to the Hills and make your everlasting fortune. But I'm not going to help anybody's boy off on such a wild-goose chase."

"Then you will not sell me a ticket?" said Phil, sulkily.

The rest of the agent's remarks seemed to have made very little impression on his mind. He did not deny that he had run away, and the agent answered him, shortly—

"No! You just go home, and stay there for the next six or eight years, and get all this nonsense out of your head. That's my advice to you."

It was very good advice, too; but Phil did not thank him for it.

He left the office disappointed and angry, and was going away disconsolately, when a remark reached his ear, uttered by one of two men who were standing in front of the poster—a remark which caused him to pause and turn an eager gaze upon the speaker.

"If you want to go cheap, Nick, you'll never get a better chance. You'd better take the ticket."

"What makes you so anxious to sell it? Thought you was bound to go, anyhow?" said the very needy-looking individual addressed as Nick.

The other replied, with a half-laugh—

"So I was, but circumstances alter cases. Things have happened since I bought the ticket that has made me change my mind. Come, now, I'll let you have it for two pounds—that's cheap enough!"

"Yes, that's cheap enough," assented the seedy Nick. "But, you see, I ain't got the money."

Here Phil stepped forward.

"I will give you that for it," said Phil, quickly.

"All right! The ticket is yours," said the young man, with equal promptness.

He never stopped to reflect that the boy might be running away from his home, and perhaps would not have hesitated to sell him the ticket if he had, being anxious to get back a part of the money he had paid for it, and not being as conscientious as the agent in the office.

"Here it is—coupons attached, all correct," said he, handing Phil a strip of yellow-brown paper, which might have been far from correct, and he still would have taken it without suspicion, for he knew nothing at all about the "coupons."

He paid over the money and went off with his prize, highly elated and in a great hurry, for it wanted now but little more than half an hour of the time for the train to start on which his ticket would be good, and he was fearful that he should be too late.

However, by making haste, he reached the station with a few moments to spare ; and, a little later, behold our impetuous Phil seated in a train and rushing out of Natal as fast as he had entered it scarcely two hours earlier.

CHAPTER V.

BOB.

HE journey of Phil was diversified by no event beyond the ordinary incidents of railroad travel. But though everything he saw was new, and under any other circumstances would have interested him greatly, he had never taken so unpleasant and wearisome a trip in all his life before.

It was not alone that the party with whom he had undertaken to travel proved to be the hardest and roughest lot of men whom he had ever found himself among—a drinking, gambling, swearing set, who shocked his noble nature with their coarse profanity, and disgusted his gentle breeding with their utter barbarian selfishness and their disregard of the decencies of life—a worse party than was often collected even for an expedition to the Dark Hills.

But everything comes to an end in time, and so at last the first stage of the long journey was finished by the arrival at a small town, where the party were to procure outfits and supplies for the Dark Hills.

They arrived in the morning, and the whole party repaired for lodging to a long, low, wooden structure, which looked as if it might formerly have been used for some other and less pretentious purpose, but now it was painted smartly, and designated in gilt letters over the door as "Smith's Hotel."

A placard further made known that the proprietor engaged to furnish the best entertainment to be had in the place for the money.

The party had but little time, however, to enjoy Mr. Smith's hospitality.

It was found that a waggon-train would leave on the following day for Red Cloud, carrying supplies for troops stationed there, and several of the waggons were engaged to go on to Deadwood with freight for the miners and others.

All who were going to the mines availed themselves of this opportunity, and preparations were hurried through as speedily as possible.

It did not seem like a very difficult piece of business, for he had seen at least half-a-dozen shops which displayed signs advertising " Mining outfits bought, sold, and exchanged," or " Miners' supplies constantly on hand."

But he did not know what he would need, nor what he ought to pay, and there was not one among the companions of his journey whom he would trust to give him fair advice or honest assistance.

The proprietor of Smith's Hotel, though he was by no means elegant of manner or speech, had a good-natured face, and looked more reliable than the others, and Phil therefore applied to him.

" Mr. Smith," said he, " will you tell me the best place to get what I want ?"

" Yes, if you'll tell me what you want," replied the host, smiling, and regarding Phil with some curiosity.

" I'm afraid I hardly know myself," said Phil, with a faint smile. " I am going to the Hills with the rest, and I suppose I want the regular outfit. Perhaps you will be kind enough to advise me what to get ?"

Smith gave a whistle of amused surprise.

" What !" he exclaimed. " You don't mean to say you want a miner's outfit? You ain't going into the hills to dig, I hope ?"

" Certainly !" said Phil, colouring, and trying to look offended at the question.

" Well, I am blowed !" muttered the landlord, under his breath.

Then, perceiving that Phil's blue eyes were beginning to flash in earnest, he said, in a bluff, good-humoured way—

" Don't get wrathy ; you've a perfect right to go to the Hills, if you like, I s'pose. But you ain't very rugged for a miner. Ain't you afraid you'll find it more'n you're counting on ?"

"It may be hard at first," answered Phil, touched in a moment by his tone of kindness, "but I shall get used to it."

"Maybe you will," said Mr. Smith, doubtfully. "I hope so."

"Thank you !" said Phil. "And about the articles that I must have—"

"Guess you'd better have somebody go with you and help you make up your outfit," suggested the kindly host. "If you don't you'll get cheated out of your eye-teeth. There's a boy here that's going with the waggon-train to-morrow ; mighty smart youngster ; knows all the ropes, and he's honest, too—I've found that out. He's been here waiting for a chance to go to Deadwood."

And, lifting his voice, he shouted—

"Bob ! I say, Bob !"

In response to this summons a boy presented himself, who looked at least two years older than Phil.

He was, in reality, several months younger, but so tall in stature and stout in limb, with such visible strength in his broad shoulders and muscular brown wrists that one would have taken him to be twenty.

No one saw anything at all surprising in this boy's notion of going to the dark Hills, though they laughed and looked astonished when Phil declared his purpose—Phil, who was really the elder of the two—for Phil was slim and fair, and hardly looked his age ; but Bob was strong enough and big enough to be counted as a man in almost any undertaking.

He was decidedly good-looking. If a figure straight and upright as a Sioux brave ; a noble head, with a broad brow and masses of dark-brown hair ; a clear, healthy skin, tanned by free exposure to sun and air to something darker than its natural shade ; keen, dark eyes, and a firm but pleasant mouth, inclosing two unbroken rows of sound, white teeth—if these things constitute good looks, then Bob was certainly a handsome boy.

He was dressed roughly enough, but his coarse blue shirt, belted with a strip of raw hide, could not conceal the grace and vigour of his fine athletic form, and his old felt hat seemed even to take a certain air of style from the jaunty way in which he wore it.

His behaviour corresponded with his dress—free and easy, a little too rough, but not in the slightest degree offensive to good morals or good manners.

Phil liked him at first sight, and trusted him implicitly from the very first moment of their acquaintance.

"Here, Bob," said Smith, "here's a young gentleman "—he laid some emphasis on the words—"who is going to the mines, and he don't understand about the outfit. You just go along and show him what's wanted, and do the best you can for him."

"All right, sir."

And Bob turned to the " young gentleman " with a cheerful nod, to which Phil responded by offering to shake hands.

Bob accepted this courtesy with a frank and hearty smile, which showed his handsome teeth ; and the two boys went out together—friends for life.

Smith followed with a meditative glance, and remarked, decisively—

"That little chap belongs to swell-folks. He's run away from his friends, I allow, and he'll be coming back from the Hills in about a month, used up and ready for home."

As for Bob, he would take care of himself, and come back from the Hills when he was ready, or not at all. Smith troubled himself very little about Bob.

CHAPTER VI.

OFF FOR THE DARK HILLS.

GUIDED by Bob, Phil took his way down the principal street of the " city," feeling encouraged and cheered by the mere presence of this bright, robust, reliable companion; but he observed that Bob kept glancing at him with surprised and curious looks. Being by this time sufficiently familiar with that sort of regard to understand its meaning very well, he got a little out of patience, and demanded—

" Why do you keep looking at me in that kind of way ?"

He knew well enough what Bob was going to say.

"Didn't mean to give any offence," said Bob, apologetically. "I was only wondering what under the canopy such a fellow as you is going to do in the Dark Hills!"

"That's what everybody wonders!" exclaimed Phil, indignantly. "I don't see why you need to find it so funny. You are going yourself—so the hotel-keeper said."

"Oh!" said Bob, with immense expression, "I'm another sort of Higgins!"

Phil turned a glance of admiration upon his stalwart young guide, and said, with a sigh—

"So you are! I wish I was half as big and stout! Then you are going, are you?"

"Yes," said Bob. "I am hired to drive a waggon to Deadwood, and I'm going to stay and try my luck in the diggin's."

"Well, I'm glad of that," said Phil, in accents of devout thankfulness. "There will be one person that I can keep company with They're such a horrible set!" he added, with a shudder of disgust.

"Pretty hard crowd," assented Bob. "I was wondering what you was doing amongst 'em."

"I knew nothing about the party before I started," replied Phil. "Never saw one of them until I got on board the train. I have avoided them as much as possible, and so I mean to. I need not have so much to do with them, I suppose."

"I don't know about that," said Bob, gravely.

And he thought to himself—

"What a green one he is! He can't get along a week without help from somebody."

Perhaps Phil divined his thoughts, for he was silent a little, and finally said, looking wistfully into the dark eyes of his guide—

"If you are going, why can't you and I keep together?"

"Pardners?" said Bob, smiling. "Well, I'd like it, but I haven't any money to pay for an outfit, so I shall have to get along the best I can with only my two hands."

He held them up as he spoke—strong, shapely members, that justified the touch of pride in his self-reliant gesture—and Phil involuntarily glanced at his own white, slender fingers, and blushed at the comparison. He took out his pocket-book, and placing all his money in Bob's hand said—

"Is that enough to buy what is needed for us both? It is all I have, and I think your two hands are worth much more."

"You're putting a good deal of confidence in me," said Bob, with a pleased smile.

He ran over the amount of money and said—

"Here's enough to buy the outfit for us two, and a little to spare. But you better think twice about it. You may want the money yet."

"I would give twice as much if I had it, sooner than lose the chance of keeping you with me," answered Phil.

Indeed, he found a sense of rest and support in the company of this alert and fearless lad, which was very grateful to him, so sick and weary and doubtful of the future.

Phil was getting his eyes opened very fast, and he began to realise that he would want a friend.

"All right," said Bob. "Just as you say. It's a good chance for me, you know, and I'll try to be as useful to you as the money would. Give you my word, I'll stick by you through thick and thin, as long as my name's Bob!"

*The head of the mad-
man was muffled in
the   blanket   in   a
moment.*

Phil's eyes brightened with pleasure.

"Thank you !" he responded, warmly. "Is your name Robert ?"

"Yes.   Robert Spencer."

"Mine is Phil Farren."

"But I always go by the name of Bob."

"And I go by the name of Phil."

"Well, we'd ought to be good friends," said Bob, laughing. "Here's the place we want. You can do as well here as anywhere," he added, turning to enter an establishment where they dealt in the various articles included under the general head of "mining supplies."

Phil was rather surprised to see what a number of different things were comprehended in that term, and he looked on with interest and curiosity, while Bob bargained for mining tools, cooking utensils, blankets, and provisions, with a business-like method which made it very evident that he "knew the ropes," as Smith said.

When he had finished the business, arranged for the delivery of his purchases, and paid for them, he offered Phil what was left of the money ; but Phil shook his head, saying—

"No, you keep it, Bob. You shall be be cashier, for you know how to manage, and I don't. I should not have thought of half the things you got. But why didn't you think of a tent? I should suppose we would want one."

"Costs too much," answered Bob. "We'll have a cabin—that's better—and it won't take us half a day to build one."

"Well ; but why did you buy all that flour and bacon and sugar and stuff? Can't you get anything to eat at the diggings ?"

"Why, yes, you can get provisions at Dead-wood," answered Bob, "but they cost all creation, and it's the best way to take a stock along with you. Now I'll speak to the boss and have them things stowed into my waggon, and you can ride when you want to. You don't look like much of a walkist."

"I don't know," said Phil, dubiously. "I suppose I can walk a reasonable distance."

"Well, this ain't a reasonable distance," smiled Bob. "It's a hundred miles and over; so I'll fix it with the boss for you to ride. I guess he won't charge much."

"Who is the boss?"

"Ned Kelly, his name is. He makes a business of carrying freight to the Hills. He's taking seven waggons to Deadwood this time. There will be twenty-five or thirty waggons at the start, but the rest of them don't go any further than Red Cloud."

"Where is that?" asked Phil.

"It is about fifty miles this side of the Dark Hills," answered Bob—"the Red Cloud Agency, you know. There's a lot of soldiers there, and a good many ranches along the route and they get all their supplies by waggon-trains. There's a mail once a week between here and the Red Cloud, and they run a stage when there's any passengers; but they go by Laramie-road, and we ain't going that way. It's twenty miles further, you see."

"Have you ever been to the Hills? You seem to know all about the routes," remarked Phil.

"Oh! you pick up all these things in a day or two," said Bob, "and I've been loafing around here this three weeks, looking out for a chance to get to the diggin's."

"Where did you come from?" Phil enquired.

" From England," replied Bob.

" I wonder if he has run away, too ?" thought Phil. And he asked, with some hesitation—

" Have you no parents or friends ?"

" None to speak of," said Bob, coolly. " My folks come from the old country when I was a small chap, but they didn't get along very well, and my father died about five years ago. After that my mother took in washing, and I did what I could to help, till I got big enough to work by the day, and then I got good wages. We were doing pretty well, but mother, she went and got married again, and then there wasn't room in the house for me. The old man didn't like me, you see, and one day he undertook to give me a whaling. *He didn't do it!*" said Bob, with trenchant emphasis. " I showed him some high old science, now you bet ! But mother, she struck in, and went for me with the broom, and so I bounced. Can't stand out against your mother, you know."

Concluding thus, he looked at Phil, as much as to say—

" It is your turn now."

Phil felt ashamed of himself, and he was sure that such a boy as Bob would not approve of his headstrong action. So he hesitated a little, and finally said—

" The cause of my coming was something like that—at least, I ran away to escape a flogging that I hadn't deserved. I'll tell you all about it, some time."

" All right," responded Bob, with his favourite formula.

And promptly changing the subject, he began to talk about the journey to Deadwood.

If he was hurt because his confidence was not returned he did not show it ; but if Phil had told his clear-headed new friend all about the manner of his leaving home, this history of his wanderings might have been sooner ended.

They returned to the hotel, and Bob left Phil at the door, explaining that he had to go and see "the boss." He said, as he was going—

"Guess you better stay with me to-night. If you don't, you'll have to take a bed in the big room, with three or four of them roughs, and you wouldn't like that."

"No," said Phil

"I've got a little corner all to myself, up in the oft. It ain't palatial," said Bob, with a grin, "but it's quiet. You'll be able to sleep up there."

"Thank you!" said Phil, gratefully. "I was dreading to pass the night among those men. They are so noisy, and I am not very well."

He spoke inadvertently, for he had meant to keep all his aches and ills to himself and make no fuss about them.

Bob looked at him keenly, and said—

"I thought there was something the matter with you. Your eyes look queer, and you are too white."

"Oh ! it's nothing of any account," said Phil, hastily. "Only I got wet a little and took cold the night I started."

He had no idea of telling Bob how ill he suddenly felt ; but, in fact, he felt scarcely able to stand.

However, he slept with Bob that night, and slept well ; and he awoke in the morning with a resolution that he would not be ill.

Bob had risen long before and gone away without disturbing him, and he could hear an uproar going on below, from which he judged that the teams which were to start from Smith's, under the direction of Ned Kelly, had arrived and were loading up.

He got up and dressed, trying his best to make nothing of the cold chill that whitened his lips and shook his hands and to ignore the throbbing pain over his eyes; and, though it was hard work, he succeeded in making himself believe that he should conquer his illness by sheer force of will and pluck, and be all right in a day or two.

He went down and found that the waggons were nearly loaded and the horses were put to them.

Bob was hard at work, but he found time to give Phil a cheery greeting and ask him if he felt better.

"Ye-es, I believe so," hesitated Phil.

He wished to believe so, at least.

"There's nothing like a good snooze for a cold. I thought you'd sleep it off!" said Bob, encouragingly. "You'd better get your breakfast and come along; we're going right away. I've got everything fixed, and you're to ride in my waggon. Mr. Kelly, this is my pardner," he added, laughing, and presenting Phil to the "boss."

Kelly gave the boy a civil nod and a curious stare, observing that Bob was a good fellow for him to hitch hosses with.

He turned away, with the additional remark that they were going to get off in just fifteen minutes.

There was no occasion for the carrying out of this threat, however, for the business of getting ready was finished in something less than the specified fifteen minutes, and with more profanity and cracking of whips the waggons were started, and they were off for the Dark Hills.

CHAPTER VII.

A FRIEND IN NEED.

AMID the excitement of the start and the cheerful contagion of Bob's good humour, Phil almost forget his pains and felt something like himself again.

A little way out of Cheyenne they joined the train which was going to the Red Cloud Agency, and they now numbered thirty waggons.

Phil thought this was quite an imposing procession; but Bob told him that it was a common thing for trains to leave the town with several hundred waggons.

" How long does it take to get to the Dark Hills ?" asked Phil.

" About six days, if you have good luck," said Bob.

The train moved on through a picturesque and wild region, stopping each night near the ranch of some stockman, or the cabin of some venturous pioneer.

On the fourth day they reached the Red Cloud Agency, fifty miles from the Dark Hills, as Bob informed his friend ; and here the principal part of the waggon-train remained, while Kelly's seven teams, with the mining party, went on to Deadwood.

Up to this time, Phil had felt pretty well ; but on the first day after leaving Red Cloud his dull headache returned, and he began to feel curiously weak, as if the strength which had kept him up so far had suddenly been taken away, and, before the third day reached its close, he found it impossible longer to conceal his state from Bob.

He was obliged to confess that he was very sick.

He was so faint, and looked so ghastly pale, that his friend was thoroughly alarmed ; but, keeping his anxiety to himself, Bob said—

"You just lie down in the waggon, and let me cover some blankets over you, and see if you can't go to sleep. We shall get to Deadwood some time to-morrow, and we'll find a doctor there to see to you. I reckon you've got a touch of the chills."

He got out a quantity of blankets, rolled one of them up for a pillow, and made the sick boy lie down on the waggon-seat ; for there was no other place, the body of the waggon being piled up to the top with its load of freight.

Even when Bob had done his best this was not a very easy position ; but poor Phil appreciated the kindness of his good-hearted companion, and tried to appear comfortable for his satisfaction.

They camped that night at Rapid Creek, some thirty miles from Deadwood, where there was quite a settlement of miners' cabins, for this place had been very popular, and numerous mining claims had been taken up.

Numbers of gold-seekers still remained in the Rapid Creek district, but many had gone to the new "diggin's" around Deadwood, and left their cabins standing empty.

Bob took possession of a deserted shanty, kindled a fire, and filled one of the rude bunks with clean straw, to make a bed for Phil, who was still lying on the waggon-seat, and was too weak to get down without help.

Bob almost carried him into the cabin, and would not leave him until he was undressed and comfortably covered up in the bunk.

"There," said Bob; "now I've got to go and look after the horses, but I'll be back pretty quick, and get you something hot to drink, and I guess you'll be all right in the morning."

Phil pressed his hand, saying, faintly—

"You are very good to me, Bob."

"Course! Ain't we pardners?" said Bob, cheerfully.

But it was a very anxious look that he gave Phil as he left him.

He told Kelly that he thought Phil had an attack of chills and fever, and the "boss" gave him a bottle of "hot drops," which he declared to be an infallible remedy.

But when Bob returned to the cabin, he found, to his relief, that Phil was sleeping heavily.

"I won't wake him. That'll do him more good than the medicine," thought Bob, who seemed to believe that sleep was a cure-all for every kind of ill.

He prepared his coffee and ate his supper alone, and after making sure that Phil was in need of no further attention, he made up his own bed in the remaining bunk and went to sleep.

Bob was tired, and he slept soundly and long. He was awakened at daybreak by a strange confusion of voices, and springing from his bunk, he saw in a moment that something was wrong with Phil.

He was rolling his head from side to side and talking aloud—a stream of words without connection or sense ; his eyes were wild and glittering, and his face and neck were flushed to a deep, burning crimson.

Bob comprehended that the boy was in a state of high fever and delirium.

And Ned Kelly was pounding on the door of the cabin, and shouting—

"Bob—you Bob ! are you going to lay there all day ? It's time we was off !"

Bob unfastened the door and threw it open.

"Don't jaw, Ned Kelly. For Heaven's sake, come and look at Phil ! He's raving—clean out of his head !'

CHAPTER VIII.

AT RAPID CREEK.

KELLY had opened his mouth to "jaw," but, at the sight of Bob's flushed face and the sound of his startled voice, the really good-hearted man came into the cabin, and, casting a glance at Phil, exclaimed—

"My gracious ! It's a fever that's on him !"

Bob stood in silence, gazing at his sick friend.

"What in creation's going to be done with him ?" muttered Kelly.

"He can't go with the waggons," said Bob.

"I guess not !" responded Kelly, with emphasis. "We'd get run out of Deadwood in a hurly if we was to bring a case of fever into a place."

One of the waggon-drivers, passing by the door

and hearing the voice of the "boss," had stopped
and looked in ; and now another driver and three
or four of the gold-hunters came up to see what was
going on.

They heard Kelly's remark, and the word "fever"
took instant effect upon them.

Fearful of contagion they fell back from the
cabin-door in haste, and stood looking on from a
safe distance.

"Well, then, you'll have to get one of them
fellows to drive the waggon the rest of the way,
Kelly," said Bob. "I'm going to stay with him."

"Can't you fix it any other way ?"

"No," answered Bob, with decision. "I don't
believe there's anybody here that would take care
of him ; and, if there was, I shouldn't leave him.'

"Don't you be a fool, Bob !" called out one of
the men from outside. "It's the yellow fever he's
got."

"It's typhoid !" said another.

"Small-pox, like enough !" cried a third.

"It ain't no such thing," said Bob. "And sup-
posing it is ? He ain't going to be left here alone
—not if I know it !"

"Then you're bound to stay ?" said Kelly.

"I am, you know."

"Well, I s'pose I hadn't ought to say anything
to hinder you," remarked the "boss," soberly.
"'Twould be pretty rough to leave him. You're a
mighty good fellow, Bob, and no mistake ! But
ain't you afraid the fever's catching ?"

"*Afraid !* Course not !" said Bob, with great con-
tempt. "I ain't that kind of a fellow ! But I don't
know what to do for him," he added, He'd
ought to have a doctor."

"I saw a doctor at Spring Creek when we come through there," said Kelly. "He'd just come to the diggin's, and had a case of medicines with him."

"That's only eighteen miles," said Bob, brightening up a little. "Think I can find somebody to go that far, or I can go myself. Phil ain't going to die——not if I can save him. He——he seems kinder near to me, you know."

There was a slight check in Bob's firm tone, and his lip trembled as he bent over the helpless boy.

Kelly wrung his hand and said again—

"You're a good fellow, Bob. But I've got to be going. I hate to leave you so ; but we must get to Deadwood before dark, and it's a good many miles. I shall be along back in a couple of weeks."

"All right," replied Bob. "I'll come out and see to unloading our things—Phil's and mine."

A little later Kelly and his company were on the way to Deadwood, and Bob was left alone with his fever-stricken friend.

The next day Bob got the loan of an old hand-cart, on which he placed Phil, and pluckily wheeled him to where the doctor lived.

Spring Creek was not much of a place for gold, but a few miners still held out there, and a rather dissolute person, who was, however, an educated man, who was known as "Doctor" Sam, resided there.

He was very kind to Phil, and insisted on having him in his own house so that he might give him full attention.

Phil was in need of it, also of Bob's nursing. After four days he felt the benefit of the care he received.

He got better, but was still very weak. Nevertheless, he wanted to go on, for time was precious to both the boys.

"We want to make our fortunes, doctor," he said.

And the doctor smiled in a quiet way that was not exactly encouraging.

"I hope you will," was all he said, "and when you've done it come back and pay me."

They could not induce him to take anything in the way of payment, and he insisted on giving them some medicine from a handsome brass-bound chest, strangely at variance with the rest of the furniture of the place.

He also possessed a gold watch which he wore, and shyly told the boys was a relic of his "early days."

The boys went on, getting a lift in a waggon that was going to a place called Rapid Creek, where they were told they could get some work to do helping the miners, who would pay them handsomely.

This, of course, they did not intend to do, for they purposed working themselves for the fortune of which Phil dreamt so much, and which was as yet far—far away.

Kelly, deprived of the services of Bob, as we said, went on alone. Under the circumstances he would not grumble, but passing through Rapid Creek he must have spoken of the boys, for on their arrival they were received by one, Jake Bliss, who welcomed them in the name of the sparse community.

"Some people have lost heart in this place," he said. "I haven't, and I don't see why I should. It isn't Paradise, however."

Phil was still very weak, and to work at gold digging for a few days at least was out of the question. He wanted to do it, but Bob said "No."

"You've got to rest," he said.

There were only about forty miners in the place, and huts for a hundred, many of the latter being deserted by those who had not found Rapid Creek pay.

Jake Bliss told the boys they could pick and choose any out of them, and they selected one which in the rough way of their country was fairly well finished.

"Now the first thing for me to do is to make up your bed," said Bob, "and there you'll be until I tell you to get up again."

Phil had ten days' entire rest, during which Bob had a look round. He did not think much of Rapid Creek, but thought it was "bettern nothing."

"Any way," he said, "there some of the men here going prospecting to-morrow, and I mean to go with 'em. I shall soon tell if we are getting on the tracks of a gold country or not."

On the morrow Phil was well enough to get up and dress, so that he could see his friend off with the exploring party, which consisted of half-a-dozen sturdy miners.

The rest of the community saw them off, giving them a parting cheer, and then went to work. Phil had a very quiet day all to himself, just moving about, and in the afternoon, feeling tired, lay down in his bunk to have a nap. He soon fell asleep, but not for long.

He was awakened by the bursting open of the door, and, starting up, he beheld a wild, haggard-faced man staring about the place.

He was of the miner class, but seemed to have recently been ill, and, without a doubt, he was mad.

This unexpected apparition naturally gave Phil a bit of a shaking, and he had not the nerve for the moment to get out of his bunk.

"Gold—gold!" cried the madman. "I *must* have it!"

He glared around the hut again, and at last his eyes encountered Phil.

"Give it up!" shouted the madman, fixing his eyes, with their crazy, covetous glare, upon Phil's bright, shining curls. "I want that gold upon your head! I want it! It all belongs to me!"

And he stretched out his hands as if to clutch the fancied treasure.

Phil shrank back with a shudder; but he had sense enough to conceal his alarm and face the maniac with as bold a front as he could assume.

"It is not gold," he said, in a steady voice. "You are mistaken—it is nothing but hair!"

"It is gold, I say!" the mad miner shrieked. "Look how it shines!"

Phil answered, as calmly as he could—

"That is only the sunshine; there is no gold about it."

"Ha! ha! ha! I've heard that before," cried the other, laughing wildly. "All is not gold that glitters, they tell me; but I know better. You can't cheat me with that story. It is *gold*, and I will have it! I tell you I'll have it—I'll have it!"

Those wild eyes glared upon him and the claw-like fingers snatched at his hair. He could no longer keep up his pretence of coolness.

Dodging out of the way, he suddenly caught up the blanket on which he had been lying, and thrust it in the madman's face, muffling his head and hands for a moment.

Such an unexpected mode of attack caused him to fall back a pace, and Phil darted toward the door.

But the lunatic was too quick for him.

Getting rid of the muffling blanket, he was after the boy in an instant, and caught him before he reached the door.

Phil struggled to free himself, and shouted for help, though he had little hope that anyone would hear, for it was not yet time for the miners to come from their work.

He struggled without avail, for he was as helpless as an infant in the grasp of the madman, whose hand was twisted in his curly hair, and whose eyes seemed to glitter with a wilder frenzy, as he gave vent to his triumph in a maniac yell.

"Ho, ho! Did you think you would escape and carry off the gold? I tell you I mean to have it if I take your head with it!"

"He will kill me," thought Phil, with a thrill. "Oh! I wish Bob would come! Bob —Bob!"

He called Bob's name instinctively, and without any thought that his friend was near; but his cry was echoed by a startled shout in Bob's own voice—

"Yes, I am here. What is the matter, Phil?"

And, with a crash of heavy footsteps, Bob rushed in, saw what the matter was, and hurled himself upon the madman like a young avalanche.

The maniac instantly let go his hold of Phil and turned to grapple the newcomer.

But when he beheld the tall, vigorous form of the lad who confronted him, he retreated, seeing, with

The officer drew back
and stared at Bob
for several seconds.

that sort of wary shrewdness which sometimes distinguishes the insane, that Bob would be a match for him.

Uttering a howl of fury, he ran out of the cabin and dashed off down the creek.

"Phil, are you hurt?" inquired Bob, anxiously. "What was he after, anyhow? What'd he want to touch you for?"

"Why, he wanted to steal my hair," replied Phil, laughing.

He was very pale, and his lips trembled, but he did not wish Bob to think him weak, and so he tried to laugh.

Bob stared at him, and repeated, in astonished accents—

"Wanted to steal your hair?"

"It is the crazy miner which Kelly once told us about, I suppose," explained Phil. "At any rate, he took my hair for gold, because it looked yellow. I wish to goodness it would turn dark. The idea of a fellow having a tow-head like a girl at my age!" said he, with great disgust. "But didn't he pull it, though! He said he'd take my head off, and it feels as if he had tried."

He felt his head rather gingerly as he spoke, and Bob said, in a tone of relief—

"Then he ain't hurt you no other way?"

"Oh! no; I am more frightened than hurt," said Phil, lightly; but turning grave in a moment, he added—"I don't know what he would have done, though, if you had not come, Bob. You are always at hand to help me, old fellow."

"I come back sooner'n I thought I should. Lucky it happened so," said Bob. "He might ha' burt you. Where'd he go, I wonder?"

And he went to the door and looked searchingly up and down the creek and all around the settlement, but the crazy man had disappeared, and was seen no more in Rapid Creek.

CHAPTER IX.

FAREWELL TO RAPID CREEK.

BOB, explaining how he chanced to return so much earlier than he had expected, said that he had left the prospecting party about midday, and had come back without delay.

"For I made up my mind," said he, "that they wasn't going to strike anything better'n there is here ; and if they don't, they're talking about making a start for the Wolf Mountains. Jake Bliss, he come back, too."

Jake Bliss owned a "claim" on the hillside above the cabin occupied by Phil and Bob.

He had informed Bob, soon after their arrival, that mining in Rapid was hard work and poor pay, and that he had considerable notion of leaving. His "pardner" had gone to Deadwood. and he found it pretty slow working the claim alone.

"Jake don't like Rapid," continued Bob, "but he don't want to go so far as the Wolf Mountains. He said he'd try it here a spell longer, and you and me could help work his claim."

Now the fact was that Mr. Jake Bliss had offered Bob a half-interest in his claim if he would take the place of the departed "pardner" and share the work and the profits equally.

Jake would have laughed at the idea that Phil's labour could be worth anything ; but Bob included his friend in the arrangement as a matter of course, knowing that Phil's sensitive pride would be hurt to find himself regarded as entirely useless.

" He said he'd go halves with us, and I s'pose we could make enough in a couple of weeks to take us back," said Bob. "Of course, I told him we wasn't going to stay—or you wasn't—and I should go back with you, anyhow—"

"Bob!' cried Phil, interrupting him, "do you mean to say you are thinking of going back to the border town with me, and then coming back here ?'

"Why, yes," answered Bob. " I s'pose it's as good as anything I can do. I can earn my living here, I guess, and that's what I've got to do some-where ; might as well be at Rapid Creek as any other part o' the world. It's a rough life, and hard work, I know, but then I'm rough and hard work ain't going to hurt me."

Phil, in answer to all this, placed his hands on Bob's shoulders, and giving him a little shake, by way of emphasis, exclaimed—

" Bob Spencer, you are going back with me if we go at all !"

" I don't see how I can, Phil."

" You could see a way for me to go?"

" Yes," said Bob, smiling. " Ned Kelly will lend

you the money, because you can pay it back, but I can't, you see."

"Why, my uncle will settle with Kelly for us both, if he will let us have the money," said Ph'l.

Bob shook his head, colouring slightly, as he returned—

"I couldn't agree to that, nohow, Phil. Your folks might think I wanted to sponge on 'em, just cause you and me was friends. I couldn't stand that, you know."

Indeed, nothing could have induced Bob to borrow money for himself, since he had no means of repaying it, and his manly spirit would not permit him to place himself in the position of expecting a return from Phil's friends for anything he had done to aid the boy. But Phil was disappointed, and he said, reproachfully—

"I don't believe you want to go, Bob. You'd rather stay here in the hills."

"No," said Bob, earnestly. "It ain't that, Phil. I ain't in love with the Dark Hills, not by a long chalk. If I'd had a home like yours, Phil—the way you told about it when you was out of your head— I'd never a' have left it for a life like this. I only come because I hadn't nowhere else to go and nothing else to do.

"Maybe you think I sha'n't be sorry to part with you, Phil; but if you think so, you don't know anything about it. I ain't the kind of fellow to make much fuss, but you've got pretty close to me since we've been together, and—I'd like to keep with you. But I don't see but we shall have to part."

"Bob, I won't part from you!"

"I don't see but what you'll have to. I'll come

and see you, though, some time," said Bob; "but it won't be till I can pay my own way."

It was very evident that he meant what he said, and that there would be no use in attempting to move him from his resolution.

Phil sighed, and murmured—

"Bob, you are too bad ! You would not talk like that if you knew how much I want you."

"Oh ! you'll live without me," Bob said, smiling ; but he added, more gravely, "I shall miss you more'n you will me, dear Phil. You'll go back to your own folks, you know, but I ain't got anybody belonging to me. We ain't got to part just yet, though ; so cheer up, Phil, and don't let's fret till the time comes. What you want to do now is to hurry up and get well and strong, or you won't be able to go when we're ready. I'm going to work with Jake Bliss in the morning, and you can take hold just as soon's you're well enough."

The next morning, Bob commenced washing for gold in company with Jake Bliss ; and in the course of a few days Phil was able to join him, and to do an amount of work which surprised Bob as well as Jake Bliss.

Indeed, he was so eager in his new occupation that Bob was obliged to restrain the ardour of his industry, for fear that he would injure himself by over-work before his health was fully restored.

Each night, the gold washed out during the day was duly divided, half to Jake and half to Phil and Bob ; and though there was decidedly no prospect of getting rich, they had the satisfaction of knowing they were doing as well as the majority of the Rapid Creek miners.

Phil, now that he had recovered his health,

speedily developed his natural propensity for getting fun out of everything.

Sometimes a fit of depression would come over him, when he was wearied with his unaccustomed toil, or when he was reminded too sharply of his far-off home.

But, in general, the gaiety of his spirits and the sweetness of his temper were really irresistible.

"Tell you what, Bob," said Jake Bliss; "that youngster ain't no slouch of a chap to have 'round. Whenever I see that yaller head of his comin' up the hill, I git my mouth made up to grin, for I know he's sure to have some sort o' fun on hand. And he works like a major, if he is slim."

"Phil ain't got a lazy bone in his body; but this ain't no place for the likes of him," said Bob, gravely. "I'm going to start him for home just as quick as we get enough of the dust."

About two weeks of this severe reality, that it seemed to Phil a very profitless employment to wash out so many bushels of dingy dirt for so few grains of gold; and he was really astonished when Bob informed him that they had amassed enough of the precious dust to defray the cost of travelling back to the coast.

Bob announced this fact one evening, as they returned to the cabin, both very tired, having worked somewhat later than usual. Phil was walking slowly, with downcast eyes, and looking rather sober, when Bob said, cheerfully—

"Well, Phil, we can start just as soon as we're a mind to, now."

Phil looked up quickly, exclaiming—

"Is that so?"

"Yes; I was reckoning up, to-day, and I see

we've got wealth enough to take us through, and
the provisions are pretty near gone," said Bob.
"Wot's left won't be any more'n we'll want to take
along with us ; so we can't stay here much longer,
anyway.   Think we better start to-morrow."

Phil's face had brightened wonderfully, but he
did not answer at once.   After a little while, he said,
looking at Bob with a wistful expression—

"Bob, don't you think, if we keep on here a couple
of months that we can earn enough to go to
England together ?"

"Why, Phil!   Homesick as you are, would you
stay here two months longer for the sake of having
me go with you ?"

"Yes," Phil answered, simply.

"And you was thinking of home just now, and
wishing you was there, I'll bet anything," said Bob,
softly.   "I know it by the look of your eyes and the
way your mouth kinder twitched."

The two boys went into the cabin and got their
supper, much more silently than was their usual
custom, and after Bob quietly began to make
preparations for leaving Rapid Creek, though there
was not much to prepare.

They would need to take with them only a
blanket and the remainder of their stock of provisions, which would be but little burden.

Bob told his friend that Jake Bliss had offered to
take their mining implements and other property,
and would pay them all that the things were
worth.

Jake had also said that if Bob came back, he
could have them again.

"We'll make an early start," said Bob, who, in
the matter of making haste to "get off," appeared

to be a good deal like Mr. Ned Kelly, "and we'll
stop at Spring Creek to-morrow night. That's as
far as you'll want to walk the first day. We can
stop at Custer City the next night."

"How far is that?" asked Bob.

"To Custer? About thirty-five miles," answered
Bob. "And from there I guess we won't be more'n
three days getting to Red Cloud. I could walk it
in less time, but you'll have to take it rather easy.
It won't do for you to get fagged out and be sick
again before you get home."

"No," said Phil.

He spoke in an absent manner, for he was re-
volving in his mind a dozen different plans to keep
Bob with him.

At an early hour on the following morning, the
youthful adventurers turned their backs upon the
rude cabin which had sheltered them for the past
four weeks and set out upon the road to Spring
Creek.

To be frank, as miners they were failures, and to
Phil there was not enough life in the business. He
talked of going home, but was he going there?

Phil looked the very picture of health now, with
his bright eyes and sun-burned cheeks and his
blanket tied up with a strap, swung over his shoulder,
while Bob carried the bag of provisions to supply
them on their journey.

Jake Bliss shook hands with them, and wished
them good luck, and they left him standing in
front of the deserted cabin, gazing reflectively
after them as they bade farewell to the Rapid Creek.

The young travellers pursued their way along the
waggon-road through a country abounding in all the
beauties of nature.

The mountain-glens were deeply shaded, the grass was moist with cooling dew, and there was life and health in every breath of the clear, fresh morning air, sweet with the fragrance of millions of flowers, and spiced with the penetrating aroma of the pines.

Travelling mile after mile amid this grand and beautiful scenery, and breathing the delightful air, Phil's heart was thrilled with a sense of joy, and contentment to think that he was at last started on his return to the beloved home he had so thoughtlessly forsaken ; and he manifested his feelings in his usual gay and demonstrative fashion.

CHAPTER X.

BORDER JUSTICE.

OB, who was affected in a different manner by these surpassing grandeurs of nature, was inclined to be quiet and thoughtful. But his gravity was compelled to give way under the influence of Phil's joyous mood, and, joining in in his merriment, * they made the wooded canyons ring with the echoes of their shouts and laughter.

"What a curious fellow you are, Phil !" said Bob, regarding his friend with a half-amused and half-admiring look. "You're as gay as a lark generally, but when you do get down in the mouth, if you don't have the bluest kind of blues, then I wouldn't say so!"

And Phil laughed.

"I want a life of adventure, something more moving than this, and I mean to get it from somewhere."

As the two boys approached the Spring Creek settlement they perceived that a disturbance of some sort was going on.

A crowd of miners and frontier roughs were shouting and gesticulating, apparently in great excitement; and, upon drawing nearer, Bob discovered that they were collected in front of the cabin occupied by "Doctor Sam."

"I hope there ain't anything wrong with the doctor," said Bob, as they hastened their steps toward the scene of the tumult.

Just as they reached the spot, a new outburst of cries arose, and several brawny fellows came out of the cabin, bringing with them a man of thirty five or forty years, whom they handled very roughly.

He was in his shirt-sleeves—a white shirt, by-the-way, and the only one in the assemblage—his hair was disordered, and he presented a generally demoralised appearance, but still he seemed superior in some respects, to the crowd who surrounded him, and Bob exclaimed—

"Why, that's the doctor himself! There's something the matter!"

He pushed his way in among the crowd, followed closely by Phil, and making a gesture to attract the doctor's attention, called out—

"Hi, doctor! what's the trouble?"

The doctor turned to look at him, and said, with a cool nod of recognition -

"Ah! my young friend from Rapid Creek. How are you? Did the sick boy get well?"

"Of course he did, and here he is," said Bob, pointing to his companion.

"But what's the matter with you, doctor? What are they going to do to you?"

"Well, I believe they propose to hang me," said the doctor.

"Hang you!" cried Bob, amazed and horrified. "What for?"

"Oh! some of these gentlemen will tell you that better than I can," returned the doctor, placidly.

Phil and Bob were both astonished at his coolness, for "some of these gentlemen" were already preparing a rope with an ugly, suggestive noose, and all eyes were turned in threatening fury upon the man for whose neck it was intended.

But the doctor, besides being really a man of nerve, probably knew that an appearance of *sang froid* would serve him best in the presence of his rude and lawless accusers.

One of them, in response to Bob's enquiring look, volunteered an explanation—

"We're doin' this thing all on the square, young feller. The prisoner's been tried and convicted of thievin' a bag of gol'-dust from a honest and hard-workin' miner, allurin' him into this ere shanty and robbin' him of his hard earnin's under a false pretence of hospertality. He pleads not guilty, in course—that's all right—but we've convicted him accordin' to law, and now we're agoin' to give him jest five minutes to own up and tell what he's done with the dust, and then we're a-goin' to string him up."

Bob stared at the speaker, and then at "Doctor Sam" with a look of absolute consternation.

"For mercy's sake, doctor!" he exclaimed, "will they hang you for that—and in this crazy kind of fashion? Why, it's awful!"

"It is the miner's justice, my young friend," said the doctor, with a sarcastic smile.

Bob, regarding Doctor Sam with a somewhat dubious look, enquired—

"But I say, doctor, can't you make a defence? You didn't do it, did you?'

"No, my lad; but I have not succeeded in convincing the court that a man does not rob himself," said the doctor, with a shrug of his shoulders, "not even when he is as intoxicated as we were last night—I and my injured friend the plaintiff, here."

He nodded to indicate a big, hard-featured and hard-fisted miner, clad in the usual flannel shirt and heavy boots.

"What, was you robbed?" asked Bob.

"No; he wasn't!" struck in the angry "plaintiff." "That's all gammon. He claims his watch was took, but I allow he's hid it away, 'long with my pouch o' dust, so's to blind this 'ere intelligent community; but he can't fool us!"

Doctor Sam remarked, composedly—

"The facts of the case, Bob—your name is Bob, if I recollect?"

"Yes, sir," said Bob.

"The facts of the case, Bob, are these— The plaintiff—by-the-way, his name is Hanks. Excuse the liberty, Mr. Hanks," said Doctor Sam, with a burlesque air of politeness.

Hanks scowled, and roughly advised him to go to a place which we will not mention here ; but the doctor responded only by an ironical lifting of his eye-brows, and resumed—

"Mr. Hanks and myself were drinking together till a late hour, and we were both of us so well set up that we can hardly be expected to give a very lucid account of what took place ; but he got out his buckskin pouch to show me the amount of gold he had gathered, and it is my opinion that he was so injudicious as to leave it in sight when we retired —he under the table and I on the top, until I rolled off and rejoined my friend on the floor.

"I have a dim remembrance of the moment when that occurred, and I believe that there was a third person in the cabin, for I had an impression of seeing a phantom-like figure flitting about, and a singular, wild face, stooping over me.

"I was not in a condition at the time to pay any attention to vagaries of that sort, but I recalled the impression in the morning when my friend, Mr Mr. Hanks, awakened me, not very gently, I assure you—insisting that I had abstracted his property and demanding restitution.

"He refused to credit my denial, even when it was found that my gold watch was gone, and also, strange to say, my medicine-chest, which I valued far more."

"That same medicine-chest you had when I was here, with all the brass fixings on it?" queried Bob, who had listened to the doctor's statement with a curious sparkle in his eyes.

"Yes," said Doctor Sam ; "it was rather conspicuous with its ornamental trimmings. But, of course, it was the contents that were valuable. I had a stock of medicines that I don't see how I can replace in this part of the world; but then," he added, dryly, "it seems that I shall not want them, according to the intentions of my fellow-citizens and the honourable court which has just passed sentence upon me."

As if to emphasise these words, a burly member of the "committee" who seemed to have charge of the proceedings here stepped forward and placed a hand on the doctor's shoulder, with the brief remark—

" Time's up !"

At these significant words, which the other committee-man accompanied by a prompt show of bringing forward the slip-noosed rope, Doctor Sam's cool composure seemed to fail him for a moment and Phil, who was tired out with his eighteen-miles' walk and had seated himself in the doorway of the cabin, uttered a low cry and turned very pale; but Bob took a quick step forward, and exclaimed—

" Hold on !"

The temporary officer of border-law was so amazed that he took his hand from the doctor's shoulder, and, drawing back, stared at Bob for several seconds before he demanded—

" What have *you* got to say about it young feller ?"

Bob rejoined—

" I've got this to say—that he never took the gold! I know who's got it."

" What ! You do ?"

" Yes," replied Bob.

And, turning to Phil, who was gazing at him in blank astonishment, he said—

" The crazy man—you know, Phil."

" Oh !" cried Phil. " Yes !"

Bob's announcement had created a great sensation, and the crowd pressed around him with excited faces and cries of—

"Go on !—Go on !"

"Who is it, youngster ?"

"Speak up, and clear the doctor !"

And Bob spoke up, in graphic language, and, with forcible brevity and a clear, distinct enunciation, gave an account of the mad gold-hunter from Deadwood, whose mania led him to appropriate anything which had the colour of gold.

A furious gesture from Phil warned him not to tell what it was that had attracted the madman to their cabin.

The fact was that the boys at school had found out—as boys at school are apt to do—that they could tease Phil by poking fun at his beautiful brown-gold hair, and the boy was very sensitive to ridicule on that point.

He was not going to have Bob give this "hard crowd" a chance to laugh at his expense. So Bob considerately omitted that part of the story.

He gave it as his opinion that the wandering maniac had come into the Spring Creek settlement —or "Hill City," as the miners called it—during the night, and, looking into Doctor Sam's cabin, had caught sight of the brass-mounted medicine-chest, and then probably he saw the watch and the pouch of gold-dust, and so "he grabbed 'em and made off. I think, if you look pretty close, you'll find some tracks of him. He seems to be following the waggon-trail right along, and I expect he'll be heard of next down at Custer or some of the French Creek places."

Acting upon Bob's advice, a search was imme-

Phil rushed forward and clutched Danton's arm frantically.

diately instituted to find any sign of the madman
having been there, and traces of his bare feet were
soon discovered in the soft loam near the doctor's
cabin.

That settled the question, for everybody there
wore boots, and Bob had described the madman
as going ragged and barefoot.

"Hanks, the plaintiff," promptly made the
honourable amend, and withdrew his charge against
the doctor.

"I 'low it's about as the boy says," he remarked ;
"and I might a' knowed Doctor Sam wasn't the
one to rob a feller-citizen—or any other man," he
made haste to add, perceiving the queer smile that
crossed the doctor's lips. "And look here, doctor,
I hope you do not bear no ill-will for this thing,
seein' as how 'twas all a mistake, and I'll make it
square with you."

"That's very handsome, Hanks, and we will call
it square," said the doctor, laughing.

Hanks then observed, disconsolately, that
they were all good friends again, but that didn't
bring back his gold, nor the doctor's watch and
medicine-chest ; adding, however, that he was
going to start right out and try to "ketch the
loonatic. There was more'n twenty ounces in that
pouch, and he didn't mean to let it go so easy."

Several others volunteered to join in the pursuit ;
but Doctor Sam declined, on the plea that his leg
was not strong enough.

"Besides, these lads have come all the way from
Rapid to see me, and I must entertain them," said
he, smiling, as he laid his hand upon the shoulder
of the boy whose quick wit and prompt testimony
had just acquitted him.

"We've come to see you, doctor, that's a fact," said Bob, "and we want to stay with you to-night; but we're going further."

"Where are you going?"

"To the coast, sir."

"You are not going to try to walk all the way?" exclaimed the doctor.

"Yes," said Bob. "Guess we can do it in three or four days without hurting Phil; he ain't much used to walking so far."

'No, I should say not; he will not stand so much as you can, Bob, too slightly built. But I am glad to see you looking so well, my boy," he added, shaking hands with Phil. "You don't look as if you had had such a hard time; but you have been pretty well pulled down."

CHAPTER XI.

THE GOAL IS GAINED.

OB assisted the doctor to get the supper, and as both the boys were hungry, as well as tired, they made a hearty meal; but the doctor ate scarcely anything. And when Bob noticed this and spoke of it, he replied that the momentous event of being tried for his life had taken away his appetite.

He talked with Phil, and learning that the boy had been at Brythewaite School, he said that Mr. Radnor was an old friend of his.

"We were schoolmates, and I used to think there never was such a good fellow as Edward Radnor," said the doctor. "So you ran away from his school, did you?"

Phil nodded, in a shame-faced way; and then, seeing that the doctor was interested, he told the whole story.

"Of course, I don't blame Mr. Radnor, sir," said he. "It was all a mistake, and perhaps he knows it by this time. But I did not see how I could stand it to be flogged."

"Would he have done that, do you think?"

"I suppose so," answered Phil.

"But you might have gone home."

"I know it," said Phil, sadly. "They would have believed my story at home. I don't know what I was thinking of, to clear out in such a heartless way."

His tone was grieved and tremulous, and the doctor saw that he felt his leaving home deeply; so he gave the boy a sympathising look, and changed the subject.

He spoke of the insane gold-hunter, and expressed the hope that the miners would do no injury to the poor unfortunate if they overtook him.

"I ain't so sure they're going to catch him," said Bob. "They won't if he goes anything like the gait he went when he left us that time. He was out of sight before you could look round."

"Did he carry off anything of yours?" enquired the doctor.

"No; but he thought he was going to make a

big haul," said Bob, glancing at his friend, and laughing.

Phil exclaimed, hastily—

"Bob, if you are determined to let that out, I will tell it myself."

So he told the doctor how the madman had threatened to take his hair, "head and all," for its golden colour; and though Bob laughed, mischievously enjoying Phil's disgust with his "towhead," as he called it, the doctor appeared to see nothing humorous in the matter.

He regarded the graceful boy with no little admiration, inwardly remarking what a fine contrast he formed to his companion, the stalwart, dark-haired Bob.

The day was nearly spent, and by the time the doctor and his youthful guests had finished their meal it began to grow dark, and Phil was glad to act upon Doctor Sam's advice and go to bed.

He was asleep within five minutes after he had bestowed himself between the blankets, but Bob did not feel inclined to follow his example at once, and he sat for a time longer talking to the doctor. They spoke in low tones, not to disturb the sleeping Phil.

"I hope you will not think me too inquisitive, Bob," said the doctor, "if I ask where you belong, and why you did not stay at home, since you are going back so soon?"

"I'm going to the coast with Phil," was Rob's reply, "and I think like enough I shall come back again if I don't find anything better to do."

Bob sighed, and spoke in a different tone from his usual steady and cheerful accents, and the doctor said, kindly—

"Then your parents are dead, my boy?"

"My father is, and my mother married again," said Bob. "So she don't want me."

"Your mother does not want you? My dear fellow, you must be mistaken."

"No sir," said Bob; "I wish I was. But the last thing she said to me was never to darken her doors again."

"Why, what have you done?" exclaimed the doctor. "Surely you are not a bad boy?"

"I don't think I am—not very bad," said Bob, with another sigh; "though I don't s'pose I've always done as I ought to. But *he* didn't like me."

"*He?* Your mother's husband?" said the doctor, beginning to understand the case. "But you don't mean to say that she discarded you to please him?"

"That's about what it amounts to," said Bob, sorrowfully. "He took a dislike to me the first time he see me, and he never give me any peace of my life. He was bound to get rid of me, and I guess mother would 'a told me to go sooner'n I did if he'd said so."

Doctor Sam wished him to occupy the other bunk, opposite to that in which Phil was sleeping; but Bob resolutely refused to keep the doctor out of his bed, and wrapping himself in his blanket, he lay down to sleep on the floor.

The doctor also retired to rest, promising to wake Bob in the morning, as he was always an early riser.

It was a needless promise, however, for they were all aroused some time before daylight by a noise at the door, and the doctor opened it, admitting Hanks and two or three of those who had gone with him in pursuit of the mad gold-hunter.

They came in soberly so that Doctor Sam at once concluded they had failed in their object.

"Hello! Hanks. So you didn't catch the crazy man?" said the doctor.

"No, we didn't ketch him," said Hanks, with peculiar emphasis. "But here's my pouch o' dust, and here's your med'cine-box—what there is left of it."

The brass-bound box was shattered out of all shape; but, owing to the velvet lining of its many compartments, the greater number of the phials they contained had escaped the breakage, and the doctor noted this with satisfaction as he exclaimed—

"Well, he has smashed it up pretty badly, that's a fact."

"It's a wonder the watch wasn't smashed," said Hanks, placing Doctor Sam's gold watch in his hand entirely uninjured. "Tell you, I was more'n astonished to find it whole. It was nothin' but jest clear luck."

"Luck!" repeated the doctor, turning over the broken box with rueful curiosity. "Why, what did he do with this?"

Hanks returned—

"He didn't do no more'n he done with himself—went over a prec'pice ninety feet high. Yes, sir.'

"Then he was killed?" exclaimed the doctor.

"Killed! I should say he was! Deader'n Julius Cæsar! We got sight of him 'bout as soon's we got over the hill; he seemed to be kinder hanging' around here," said Hanks, proceeding to relate the particulars. "But the way he put when he sees us was a caution to greased lightnin'! We chased him a good four hours, steady, and then we wouldn't 'a ketched him; but finally we brought him up all standin' at the top o' that big ledge on the south side o' Slatestone Canyon—and then we thought we had him, sure! But I'll be shot if he didn't give a yell fit to make your flesh creep—it made mine—and went clear over that there prec'-pice ninety feet if it's an inch, and all rocks at the bottom !"

Phil, who had risen up in his bunk, looked at Bob with a horrified expression, and even the doctor shuddered.

Hanks continued—

"We went round and got down there, and—found him. He was a sight, you believe! I don't see how the watch come to be whole, nor them little bottles not smashed any worse! Well, I got the gold back," said Hanks, with a sigh of relief, "and we dug a grave in the canyon, and buried the poor, loony critter."

So that was the end of one man's hunt for gold.

Hanks and his party withdrew to carry their intelligence to the rest of the interested citizens; and as it was now approaching daybreak, and they were too much excited to sleep again, Phil and Bob made ready to proceed on the next stage of their journey.

Doctor Sam, though he was loth to lose the opportune visitors who had served him so well, felt that he could do no less in return than to speed them on their way; but when they parted from him he could not conceal his feelings of regret.

The boys were well on their way at sunrise, and though the day promised to be extremely warm, Bob gave it as his opinion that they could reach Custer City by noontide, and then if Phil did not feel too tired, after resting for a couple of hours, they might go on to " Blumer's Farm," a stock-raiser's place, some seven miles further on their route.

" If we stay at Blumer's to-night, instead of Custer,' said Bob, " it'll make a shorter stretch to-morrow ; and that's worth while, for we've got to walk about twenty-five miles, after leaving Blumer's, before we come to another ranch. I believe they allow it's that far to Sacket's."

" Well, don't you think I can walk as far as that without hurting myself?" said Phil, rather indig-nantly. "You don't seem to have much opinion of me, Bob."

" I've got a tip-top opinion of your pluck," replied Bob, laughing. " And I will say you're a better walkist than I s'posed you'd be, so I guess you will get as far as Blumer's to-day."

They did indeed reach Custer City before the morning was entirely spent, and Phil declared him-self quite capable of walking as far again.

We all have failures in life, and Phil had experi-enced his first one.

Bob also admitted that he had not been " quite so lucky as he could wish ;" but they were not going to give in for all that.

" We'll ship off somewhere else," said Bob, " and see what we can do. Two such likely young fellows as us will be sure to find a captain glad of us."

Phil was not quite so sure of it.

His experience was that captains wanted sailors, and not inexperienced lads, and he told Bob as much.

But Bob did not lose heart on that account.

" I'll tell you what we will do," he said. " When

we get .to Natal we can earn a little bit of money somehow, and get a sailor's rig-out for each of us ; then a couple of chests with a few things in it will do the rest."

" But they will find us out afterwards."

" When we have got out to sea," replied Bob, "and then they will have to do the best they can with us. Why, do you think we shall be all our lives learning the ordinary duties of a seaman ?"

" I hope not," said Phil, " but we must pick upon a vessel that is not going home, as I do not wish to go there yet."

Bob was indifferent about that. One place was as good as another to him.

It was rather a long tramp, but they got to Natal at last, and then, as Bob said, they obtained work to do without much difficulty.

They hired a room, and jobbed about all sorts of things, unloading cargo, carrying messages, and what not. By living closely they saved more than a p und a week between them, and this they invested in sundry things which might prove to be useful in a life of adventure.

Among their things was a Winchester rifle each, and a fair supply of ammunition.

Both were bought from a party of miners who had returned unsuccessful from the gold fields, and some of the members were very hard up.

At last they were ready to go to sea, and they rigged themselves out to catch a captain's eye. In this they were almost immediately successful, but not exactly in the way they expected.

One day they came across a kindly-faced captain of an American vessel, who stopped and eyed them all over.

"Well," he said, "what are you two doing?"

"Looking for a ship," replied Phil, confidently.

"Oh! indeed," he said, "and no doubt you are A 1 seamen?"

The tone and manner of the man denoted the fact that they were found out, and they were walking away disappointed when he called them back.

"Have you any friends here?" he asked. "Come, out with your whole story. Do you want to run away to sea?"

He was so frank that they thought it better to tell him exactly how they were situated. He listened with a humorous smile on his face.

Phil, we ought to say, said nothing about the false suspicion which had driven him from home. He simply said he had run away "because things were disagreeable at school."

"I'll tell you what I'll do with you," said the captain. "I'm bound for Calcutta from here, and I'll take you as passengers for a trifle. You can see if you like the sort of life we have at sea. If so I'll take you on, for you are a likely pair of lads. What say you?"

And what they said was—

"Yes; and thank you."

CHAPTER XII.

CAST AWAY.

A LONG yellow line hung in foreboding prominence upon the horizon line at the close of a beautiful day in the Indian Ocean. The sea was like glass, and to a novice this would seem no precursor of a storm.

Yet every man aboard the schooner Isidore, Captain Warren Phelps, of Bucksport, Maine, was in the rigging and working as though their lives depended upon taking in sail.

That ominous yellow cloud was a fair warning to Captain Warren of the oncoming of the deadly typhoon.

Twenty minutes previous it had not been in sight. Now it was thrusting one long, sinuous arm up toward the zenith with alarming rapidity.

"Lively there—lively, all hands !" roared the bluff captain. "Belay, you lubbers ! Work, you block-heads, work !"

And the nimble tars did work. They knew quite as well as Captain Warren what depended upon quick work.

With even a rag spread, when the typhoon should strike the ship, it would mean destruction.

Down came the heavy mainsail with a boom like thunder. In an incredible space of time the mizen and royals followed.

Not much time was given the sailors, for a good deal of canvas was spread.

But they worked like spirits, clewing this sail and lashing booms, until at length the last man slid down the ratlins, and the ship was under bare poles dead before the hurricane.

"Batten the hatches !" roared Captain Warren. "Land-lubbers all below !"

"That means us," said Phil Farren.

"You are right," replied Bob. "But I want to stay on deck. Here is where all the fun will be."

"No use. The captain will kick at that. You know his ways well enough."

"I suppose so."

Captain Warren had cast a warning glance in their direction, and Phil led the way reluctantly to the cabin stairway.

The boys went below, disappointed at not being able to remain on deck.

The hatches were battened down and the boys, left to themselves, were the only occupants of the pitching cabin.

"Well, I don't like this," growled Phil. "Shut up like rats in a trap. What if the ship goes down? Our goose will be cooked."

"Hark!" exclaimed Bob. "Here comes the typhoon."

Had the boys been on deck they would have witnessed a terrifying sight.

As far as the eye could reach along the horizon a white wave crest was speeding like a race-horse. Nothing could resist that terrific cyclonic wave, and the moment it struck the Isidore she went upon her beam ends.

Captain Phelps was at the mainmast, and as a hamper of rigging came down from above with a crash he was struck upon the head by a loose block.

He dropped senseless upon the deck, and before any of the sailors could reach him a wave broke over the deck, the ship was partly submerged, and the captain and three of the crew were never seen again. This sealed the fate of the Isidore.

Appalled at the fate of the bluff Captain Warren, the remainder of the crew lost their heads.

For a brief time the wind drove through the rigging of the ship like a thousand howling demons, snapping ropes and booms, bringing the mainmast by the board.

Urged by the first mate, and impelled by the utter desperation of the thing, the terrified sailors went forward to cut away the mast.

But they had barely begun work when the ship was literally buried in a tremendous sea.

No person could live on deck at that moment. When that awful wave was past and the gallant schooner came up from under it like a cork, not a man was left to even steer the ship. Every one of the crew was past earthly redemption.

The cyclone was over almost as quickly as it had come.

It had created terrible havoc with the staunch schooner, which, dismantled and leaking badly, lay upon her side in a rolling sea.

Not a man of the crew of fourteen men was left.

At the mercy of wind and wave the Isidore drifted on in the pathway of turbulent waters left by the cyclone.

A more awful catastrophe than this could scarce be imagined.

That not one of the crew should be spared seemed like a terrible decree of fate. And the setting sun glinted its rays across the subsiding sea and over the deserted deck of the hapless schooner.

Below decks, Phil and Bob had been tumbled about like bits of glass in a kaleidoscope. Phil had ruined his clothes and dislocated (as he declared) his spine. Bob had bumped his cranium in a forced somersault and raised a swelling which bid fair to equal his head in size.

But though badly shaken and well aware of the fact that it had been a hard storm, neither of the boys dreamed of the actual casualty on deck.

It was not until after the ship lay easy and quiet, though upon her side, that Bob proposed going on deck.

"It's over, Phil," he said, joyfully. "Why the deuce don't they open the hatches?"

"Whew! how she rolls," exclaimed Phil. "I say, Bob, I don't hear anybody on deck."

"Wait a moment! I'll wake 'em up," said Bob; and he rushed to a speaking-tube which connected with a shrill whistle by the mainmast.

The result was a douche of cold water up his nostrils.

Nearly strangled, Bob abandoned this plan.

But Phil had climbed up the companion-way, and endeavoured to force open the hatch. He was unable to do so.

"I say, Bob," he shouted. "It's mighty queer that we don't hear 'em. Suppose anything has happened?"

The two boys in the dim light of the cabin looked at each other aghast. Bob was the first to act, and he raised his voice and shouted—

"Halloa! Captain Phelps. Help!"

No answer came back.

CHAPTER XIII.

WRECK OF THE SCHOONER.

SAVE for the drip of water, and the creaking of cordage, not a sound from the deck above was heard. Pale and excited, Phil exclaimed—

"I tell you, Bob, that ain't right. Something has happened, and—Great Heaven! I am almost sure they are all drowned. What shall we do?"

There was a light of resolution in Bob's eyes.

"The first thing to do," he declared, "is to raise that hatch. We must get on deck."

"Can we do it?"

"We can try."

"Right you are."

With this they put their backs to the heavy trap and bore it upward. It required their utmost strength to do this, however.

But it was accomplished, and the boys sprung out upon the deck.

A wonderful scene was spread before them.

To the westward all was a placid sea and clear sky.

To the eastward could be seen the receding storm, and in the distance the sea was lashed to fury. But the boys only gave one glance at all this.

Another spectacle was presented to them which held their interest completely.

It seemed as if a small island had arisen from the sea. Not a mile distant and off the shores of this the schooner was drifting. Waving palms and high cliffs could be seen after the manner of all tropical islands.

It was a terrible moment for Matafayo.

" Wonderful !" exclaimed Bob, with a deep breath. " Isn't that a beauty, Phil ? We must pay it a visit."

" It will be a visit of compulsion, I am thinking," said Phil, with pale face. Bob gave a start.

"What do you mean ?' he asked.

" The schooner is sinking."

That Phil had guessed the truth, a few moments of careful investigation conclusively proved.

Water was rushing into the hold of the vessel through a large gap, and she must soon sink.

Here was a decidedly dampening discovery, and to others than the two plucky lads—only survivors of the wreck—might have been most discouraging.

Only for a moment did either of them give way to depression of spirits.

It needed only a brief examination to satisfy them both of the manner in which the crew had lost their lives.

They experienced a pang of grief for the fate of Captain Phelps, whose friendship they had valued highly.

But it was not a time to give way to depression of mind, for an exigency of the most pressing sort confronted them.

The schooner was sinking, and to go down with it was by no means the inclination or desire of the boys. Self-preservation is the first law of nature, and they smothered the feeling of desolation which the fate of their companions had engendered, and gave attention to the present dilemma.

" Isn't it lucky, Bob, that we didn't stay on deck,' philosophised Phil. "We can just thank our stars for that."

"You're right, old boy. Deuce take it! I don't see a boat anywhere—do you?"

"Yes, there is the long boat."

"But it is stove in."

"There is the dingey."

"Certainly; queer I didn't see it before. Let's get our clothes, and launch her as quick as we can. We haven't any time to lose."

Bob vanished into the cabin, and Phil proceeded to rig out the dingey ready for launching. In a moments Bob reappeared with a square trunk on his shoulders.

"I thought you were after provisions," cried Phil. "Going to take your trunk?"

"Of course," rejoined Bob. "All of my clothes and other things are in it. Do you think I'd let them go down with the ship? Not much! I might as well go down myself."

"Well, I know you hold that trunk pretty dear," laughed Phil. "But if you are going to save yours, I might as well have mine. It will serve us a good turn on shore."

"But yours—"

"Has all my carpenter's tools and things, and my rifle. Suppose I'd lose that? Not much!"

And down into the cabin went Phil, presently reappearing with a big trunk on his shoulders similar to Bob's.

These were stowed away into the boat, and then it was launched.

Just in time the boys leaped in and began to row away.

They had barely reached a safe distance when the schooner, with a mighty plunge, went down..

The water boiled and surged for some while, and brought some wreckage to the surface; but otherwise than this nothing remained of the gallant schooner which an hour before had ploughed the main a staunch and noble vessel

Cast away in the Indian Ocean, adrift in the dingey, and without even provisions, the position of our boy adventurers can well be imagined.

Bob exchanged a glance with Phil, and then said, in a hoarse voice—

" Kind of rough, ain't it, Phil? I'm inclined to think we've got to play Robinson Crusoe."

If there was a big lump in Bob's throat, there was one in Phil's, too ; but neither remained there long, for Phil suddenly leaped up in the boat, crying—

" Luck ! How's that for luck, Bob ? Look—oh ! just look at that."

Bob did look, and the sight which rewarded the gaze of both boys thrilled them through and through.

Around the corner of the tropical isle a full-rigged ship had glided into view.

She had evidently escaped the typhoon, and it seemed as if an act of Providence had caused her to appear at that opportune moment.

CHAPTER XIV.

THE MUTINY.

STATELY and grand did the ship Pelican look as she turned the corner of the island at that moment, and the boys, delivered from their dubious prospects, sprang up and shouted with joy.

"Hurrah! They see us, Bob. Give 'em a yell. Hallo, the ship! Hullo!"

Phil's voice reached the ears of those on the Pelican's deck, and a response came quickly enough.

"Ahoy! the boat!"

"Ahoy!" replied Bob.

"Do you want to come aboard?"

"Yes."

The boys heard a ringing voice give orders to the crew, and then the ship's head was brought around, the high cliffs took the wind from her sails and the dingey came alongside.

A rope was thrown, and Bob took a turn around the small boat's stern-post with it, and the ship once more stood off. In a few moments they were aboard the Pelican.

The first thing which impressed the boys as they stepped on the Pelican's deck, and which they long remembered, was that the crew were the most villainous-looking set that they had ever seen.

But the captain was a tall, genial-featured man, who exclaimed, in a hearty voice—

"Well, lads, what on earth are you doing here in that light boat?"

It did not require but a few moments for Bob to tell the whole story. The crew crowded about listened with deep interest. Captain Alden, which was the name of the ship's master, said—

"I saw the typhoon. It passed us a dozen miles to windward. Well, boys, that's hard luck, but you're welcome aboard the Pelican."

"Thank you!" said Bob. "But may I ask where you are bound for?"

"Certainly. I am going to Calcutta from here. But we're out of water and I'm trying to make a landing on this isle to procure that necessity."

The boys were given hammocks in the main cabin and tried to feel at home.

But the horror of the loss of the Isidore and the awful fate of the crew was now revived in their minds, and they felt much depressed.

They saw that Captain Alden was the only kindred spirit on board.

The first mate was a ferocious-looking ruffian, named Bud Danton, and he seemed to be continually inspiring the crew with mutinous feelings.

It did not require an hour on board the Pelican for the boys to see this, and they would much have liked to tell Captain Alden their opinions, but were obliged to keep quiet.

For three days the Pelican lay off the island, then a landing was effected.

The task of bringing off the water in casks was begun. Bob and Phil embraced the opportunity to go ashore.

They found the tropical isle a bower of Eden, so far as foliage and verdure were concerned, various coloured birds sang in the forest, and animals of different species fled at their approach.

From an elevation Bob viewed the sea about, and saw that this was only one of a chain of small islands.

The boys were delighted with the beauty of the island, and returned to the ship very enthusiastic.

As they were rowing to the ship, a strange thing happened.

Bud Danton, the Pelican's first mate, was standing upon the stern of one of the boats engaged in bringing off the water casks.

He was swearing at the men like a trooper, when a very peculiar thing occurred.

One of the heavy casks, becoming dislodged, fell overboard.

Danton had made an effort to restrain it, and, losing his balance, went over too.

He went down into the water tangled up in a coil of rope. The men in the boat, whether from choice or not, made no effort to save him.

He must have drowned for a surety had it not been for Bob and Phil.

"Pull for him, Phil," cried Bob, and they turned their boat in that direction. Bob saw a part of the rope coil on the water and began pulling it in.

This brought the half-drowned man to the surface, where he was held until the other boat could return.

Had it not been for the prompt work of the boys Bud Danton must have been drowned.

For this service rendered he did not even thank his rescuers. He commenced to curse the men

again most roundly, and seemed to forget the
episode entirely.

"He is a big brute!" declared Bob.

"Worse, he is a coward!" rejoined Phil.

With these sentiments the boys returned to the
ship.

When the close of the day came and the Pelican
lay rocking at her anchors, Bob came out of the
main cabin and meeting his chum on the deck,
said—

"I say, Phil, what makes me feel so funny?"

Phil looked up in surprise.

"Why, what's the matter with you?" he asked.

"I can't tell exactly; but I feel so queer, just as
if something terrible was going to happen."

"Is that so? Well, do you know I feel the same
way."

The boys stared at each other.

"What is it?"

"What's up?"

"I can't understand it," said Bob, finally. "It
may not amount to anything, but I tell you I
believe that something terrible will happen before
another day."

"I don't see what it can be."

"Nor I. But I believe it."

The sunset in those latitudes was a wonderful
sight, and the boys enjoyed it and remained on
deck until quite a late hour before retiring.

Bob's hammock was near an open port and any
noise on the deck could be plainly heard by him.

He had now sunk into a troubled sleep, and it
must have been near the hour of midnight when he
was awakened. The sound of voices floating in at
the open port was the cause.

For the life of him, he could not have ignored the voice above the others which he instantly recognised as Bud Danton's.

Rising in his hammock he began to listen, and was accorded a startling revelation.

"Everything is all ready, is it, Jake?"

"You can bet your life it is."

"There won't be any mistake?"

"No."

"All right. You'll do the job?"

"No. Bud is going to do it."

"Are you, Bud?"

"Yes," replied Danton's harsh voice. "One stroke, boys, and the game is ours. We will run off to Java, put aboard four good cannons and some small arms, on the quiet, then—Captain Danton and fortune! With a black flag at the old Pelican's mast-head we shall sweep the seas. We shall be princes before a year has passed."

"Aye—aye!" cried a chorus of voices. "We are with you, Bud."

"Every man on board has sworn to stick to the black flag once Captain Alden is out of the way. One stroke will settle that. He sleeps in his cabin now. Wait you here."

Bob waited to hear no more. Thoroughly impregnated with horror, he was out of his hammock in a twinkling. He shook Phil, waking him up.

"Quick, Phil, for your life. They are going to kill Captain Alden. We must save him at any cost. For the love of Heaven! Quick!"

Phil Farren needed no second bidding. He sprang up also, and gasped—

"Oh! Heavens, Bob! He is dead."

"Dead!"

"Yes.

"How do you know that?"

"I just dreamed it."

"No—no," cried Bob, wildly. "Come! We must warn him in time."

They started for the cabin stairs.

But they were unable to ascend. The hatch was down. All efforts to lift it were in vain.

This was part of the scheme of the mutineers.

Bob was frantic. The captain's cabin was just forward, and there was no other way for the boys to reach it. What should they do?

And at that moment a muffled sound came to their ears which congealed the blood in their veins. A shuddering cry escaped Bob.

From beyond the cabin partitions there came a stifled, awful cry of agony, then the indistinct sounds of a scuffle, and a heavy fall.

Bob reeled back sick and faint.

"Oh! Phil," he gasped in horror. "They have murdered Captain Alden. What shall we do? Oh! what shall we do?"

It would be idle to attempt to depict with a pen the emotions of the two boys at that thrilling moment.

Not only were they bound to reflect upon the horror of the dark crime, but the utter desperation of their own position.

Who could say that their turn would not come next? Imprisoned as they were in the cabin, they were wholly at the mercy of the bloodthirsty mutineers.

Why should Bud Danton spare them? Bob asked himself this question, and then sat down upon the cabin stairs to think.

As he did so, there was the tramp of feet on the deck above, and savage yells.

The boys could hear the click of wine-glasses and hideous oaths, and knew that a carousal was being held.

It was long after sunrise when the hatch was lifted, and an evil visage peered down upon the boys.

"Ah! there ye are. Trying to git out, was ye? Well, come up and take a peep at daylight!"

The boys climbed up to the deck and emerged into the light of day to find themselves confronted by the villain Danton and surrounded by the mutineers.

But the crew of ruffians had changed vastly in appearance.

They were now armed with cutlasses and pistols, and altogether bore quite a piratical appearance.

Danton assumed a fierce expression of countenance, and said—

"I'm captain of this vessel now, you see. Captain Alden fell overboard. You'll take your orders from me."

It was evident that he made these remarks solely for the purpose of seeing what effect they would have upon the boys.

His desire was gratified.

Bob, who was a stranger to fear, turned upon him with flashing eyes.

"That is a black lie, and you know it, sir. Captain Alden was murdered by you. I know it, for I heard the whole plot as you laid it out last night."

Words cannot express the effect of this upon the

chief of the mutineers.   His face turned as black as
a thunder-cloud, and a dangerous gleam shot from
his evil eyes.

"What?" he hissed.   "You dare to talk to me in
that way, you little upstart?   Why, you forget that
your life is in my hands.   I could kill you."

"Bah!   You're a big blackguard and a coward,"
scoffed the plucky Bob.   "The law will deal with
you for this crime.   You dare not take the life of
either of us.   The world would not be so wide but
that our friends would hunt you down."

"I dare not!" repeated the villain, in tones of
thunder.   "Confound you! you impudent brat.   I
will show you whether I dare take your life or not.
Hey there, men!   Drop a line from the main yard.
Knot and loop it and make it ready for hanging.
Confound you!   You shall die."

In vain Phil had pinched Bob's elbow and tried
to restrain him in his imprudent declarations.   The
young fellow's blood was up, so to speak, and
knowing the awful guilt of Bud Danton he could
not help but give him his opinion clear and candid.

And for this he was to hang from the yard-arm.
When it seemed too late, a sickening sense of his
imprudence came to him.

He saw the lawless men reeve the rope which
was to shut off his wind for ever, and an awful
desperation seized him.   Death in its most frightful
form confronted him.

CHAPTER XV.
MAROONED.

O be hung from the yard‑arm of the Pelican was a fate which Bob Spencer had never dreamed of as his likely portion, nor did he relish the terrible prospect.

Yet he could not help but realise that he was in the power of an unscrupulous man, a veritable fiend, who would not hesitate to consummate revenge in just such a summary and frightful manner.

Yet Bob's valour was of the stubborn kind, and he would have swung willingly from the yard-arm before he would have retracted the declaration which he had made.

Phil was beside himself with horror and despair, and as the men came forward to seize his chum he rushed to the side of Danton, crying, wildly—

"Oh! you must not hang him. You shall not—it is not right. He is too young to die yet. Oh! I pray of you not to do it."

These words of appeal fell unheeded upon Danton's hearing.

"Slip the loop around his neck," he cried savagely. "Stand ready to draw when I give word."

The ferocious orders were instantly obeyed.

Bob was unable to resist.   He was a child in the *clutches of those human wolves.

The noose was placed about his neck and he stood with ashen face ready to be swung up on his impromptu gallows.

The men, obedient to the command of the villain Danton, stood by ready to draw on the rope.

"Now what do you think, young whipper-snapper?" hissed the brute.   "Do you realise that you are in my power?"

"I do realise it," replied Bob, calmly.

Phil rushed forward and clutched Danton's arm frantically.

"You must not—you must not hang him!" he cried, wildly.   "You forget that we saved your life. At least you owe us for that."

Danton gave a start and hesitated.   An impulse prompted him to say.—

"Yes, you saved my life.   I do owe you for that. But you have defied me."

"Bob spoke hastily," cried Phil.   "Really, he did not know what he was saying."

Danton gazed down into the boyish upturned face.

What motive prompted him to relax his rigid purpose at that moment it would have been hard to say.

It certainly was not that of compassion or charity or even gratefulness for the favour done him.   Of these qualities he was quite incapable.

But he drew himself up, and motioning the men back, said—

"Upon one condition I will spare your lives. You must agree to it or die."

A glad cry burst from Phil.

"What is that?" he asked, eagerly.

"This ship from to-day is a pirate ship, and the black flag will never be lowered from her masthead so long as one of her timbers floats. You must join our company and become of us. Will you do it?"

Phil moved instinctively to Bob's side. They both exchanged glances, and then, turning to their captor, said, in one voice—

"Never!"

Danton's face turned black. He seemed for a moment unable to control himself.

"Then you would rather die?" he hissed.

"Yes."

"You are a brace of fools. Fortune would be yours. I want just such plucky lads as you. Think it over."

"We will die first," said Bob.

"Then die you shall," declared Danton, angrily, turning on his heel. But he did not give the order to execute the hanging. Instead, he strode to the far end of the ship.

A sudden idea seemed to have struck him, for he returned quickly and cried—

"I have it! You are not afraid to die. Now I will offer you another alternative, which is worse than death. Do you see that island? It is a barren, desolate spot in the vast ocean. Perhaps in twenty years another ship may not sight it. You shall either agree to join our company or I will put you ashore there, without food or water, to die a lingering death. Now I reckon you'll come to terms."

The villain spoke with apparent conviction that he had at last found the right leverage.

But he was doomed to disappointment.

The boys exchanged eager glances.

The idea of being marooned on this island was by no means to them a distasteful one.

It was by all means far preferable to remaining on the pirate Pelican, under the subjection of the despotic Danton.

To be left without food was serious, but there were birds and animals and even fish to be had.

Bob, with inspiration, made reply—

"Look here, Danton. Why can we not compromise? If we do remain aboard your ship, it is by no means likely that we should work in your interests or remain in sympathy with your plans. It would be better for you to have nothing to do with us. Put us ashore on this island with our chests, and you may leave us food or not, as you please. You will then be as well rid of us as you would to kill us. Will you do this?"

Danton's face lit up oddly. Then, with a sudden decision, he said—

"You are right. It is my best way to get rid of you. I will do it."

Both boys felt like leaping in the air with joy, but restrained their feelings while the noose was removed from Bob's neck, and he was once more free.

Their spirits arose instantly.

Danton was as good as his word. A boat was lowered, and the boys with their valued chests were rowed ashore.

Unceremoniously landed on the sandy beach of the tropical isle, they watched the boat pull back to the ship, saw the anchor weighed, a black flag run up, and the Pelican, under the new *regime*, stood seaward.

Upon the ground were two bleached human skeletons.

Then Bob turned to Phil and they clasped hands.

"Are you sorry?"

"You reckon I am not."

"I think we can get a living here."

"That is better than our fate would be aboard that ship."

"You are right. Let us now take a look around."

Dragging their chests up out of the reach of the waves, they opened them and took out a couple of Winchester rifles.

Then, relocking the chests, they set out along the shore.

It was early in the day yet, and the boys knew that they had ample time to reconnoitre the vicinity. Their sensations are not easily described in words.

Would they ever see home and friends again? Both had faith that they would, and at all events, were not disposed to borrow trouble.

Anything was better than life aboard the Pelican with Bud Danton as the captain. The boys shuddered when they thought of their narrow escape.

The sandy shore of the tropical isle was as smooth as a floor to walk upon and the boys in high spirits sped along.

They started up some game birds, much like a pheasant, from tall grass in shore, and shooting a brace, provided themselves with the material for a dinner when the time should come.

Shells and coral, bits of beautiful colour, strewed the beach.

High, precipitous cliffs arose from the beach, and in crevices in their surface, scraggy bushes and palms grew out.

"I wonder if this island was ever inhabited?"

mused Phil, as he looked about in vain for some
sign of human occupation.

"I should say not," replied Bob. "At least not
by human beings."

"Shall we follow the beach any further, Bob ?"

"Just as you please."

"Let us take a look into the interior."

"All right. It is fitting that we should know
more of the place which may be our home for years,
Phil."

"So say I. Well, here goes."

With this Phil diverged from the beach, entering
a cleft in the cliffs. Suddenly he gave a great cry
of amazement.

"As I live, Bob, the isle has been inhabited, if it
is not at this very moment."

He pointed to a series of perfectly chiseled stone
steps in the wall of rock. The lapse of time had
caused them to become overgrown with moss.

Yet it was easy to ascend them, though Phil had
not taken a dozen steps upward when a viper struck
at him from a crevice in the rock.

Phil killed it with the butt of his rifle, and the boys
went up the steps.

They led up to the summit of the cliffs, where
a wonderful and startling sight met the gaze of the
boys.

To seaward a mighty extended view could be had.
Inland were seen hills and valleys overgrown with
creeping vines and wild tropical foliage.

Just in the centre of the island was a rugged rock
clad mountain with a thin blue mist like vapour
ascending from it. That it was a volcano they
rightly guessed.

All this the boys took in at a glance. Then their

attention was enchained by a nearer and more thrilling spectacle.

In a semicircle upon the table rock of the cliff, chained with heavily forged chains to nine upright pillars of granite, were nine ghastly grinning skeletons.

Horrors of horrors.

It was a maddening, terrifying spectacle, such as caused cold chills to traverse the frames of the two boys, and call up all sorts of weird, fantastic reflections.

Once, as it was easy to reflect, these nine hideous, whitened skeletons were nine living, breathing men.

Chained to those pillars of stone, undoubtedly left to linger and die by some terrible foe, what must have been the sensations of each, especially of the last, as he witnessed the death struggles of his comrades and knew that he must soon follow.

Both boys gazed at the awful spectacle for a moment spellbound.

Then Phil exclaimed—

"Good Heavens! did you ever hear of anything so inhuman as this, Sam?"

"Never."

"They are not the skeletons of cannibals, either. See !"

Phil picked up the remains of a rusted cutlass and examined it.

"That is the make of a hundred years ago," he declared. "The mild climate has preserved these skeletons or they would have been dust long ago. Only think, they must have been chained here to die at least a century ago."

But Bob, with an excited cry, had bent over a

flat stone set in the semi-circle. Upon the stone was cut with a chisel, in indelible fashion, an inscription which threw a flood of light upon the awful mystery.

———

CHAPTER XVI.

THE CLIFF HOUSE.

BREATHLESS and excited, the boys bent down over the inscribed rock set at the foot of the nine pillars of stone to which were chained the nine skeletons.

Some of the characters were clogged with moss, but with a knife-blade these were cleared out, and then the boys read—

"*A. D. 1794. Done by the hand of Captain Black. So may die all traitors. Amen!*"

Phil looked at Bob, and for some moments silence reigned.

"Do you understand it, Bob?" asked Phil at length.

"Well," replied Bob, in his methodical way, "I should say that these nine men were chained here and left to die by Captain Black, who esteemed them traitors. But who was Captain Black?"

"Why!" exclaimed Phil, suddenly. "Don't you remember that Captain Phelps told us of an old-time pirate captain in these seas whose name was Black?"

Bob's eyes shone like stars.

"That is right," he cried. "Captain Black was a noted pirate."

"Yes."

"There is not a sailor upon the high seas to-day

but can give you wonderful yarns of old Captain
Black. This is the same. What a horrible
fate!"

A fearful fate, indeed. To stand enchained there,
gazing seaward until a slow, lingering death came
as a relief, must have been a terrible thing.

For one to see another die before his eyes and
know his turn must come next must have been hard
indeed. The boys shivered and turned away from
the terrible spectacle.

"But Captain Black must have used this island
as a sort of rendezvous," said Bob, as they started
over the cliff. "Else why were those stone steps
built? If their stay upon the island was simply
for the purpose of executing the traitors they would
hardly have gone to the trouble of building the
steps."

"Undoubtedly we shall find other traces of the
pirates," rejoined Phil. "We have explored but a
small part of the island as yet, you know."

They were at the moment walking over the cliff's
vast ledges of rock, when suddenly Bob came to a
halt with a little cry of amazement.

"What is the matter?" asked Phil.

"Wonderful!" exclaimed Bob. "Do you see
that vein in the ledge? Note how it tends upwards?"

"Yes."

"Well, that is a very fine grade of lead ore. I
will warrant this isle is rich in minerals."

"Yes, but what is it worth? Nobody could ever
come here to mine it."

"It may be worth a good deal to us before we
leave this isle," replied Bob, quietly.

"What?" exclaimed Phil. "You don't mean to

say that you would think of working that vein of lead ?"

"It will all depend upon how long we remain on this isle," was Bob's reply, and with this he fell to making an examination of the vein with constant exclamations of delight.

He was an ardent student in mineralogy, and understood well the value of the rich deposit of ore.

After some time spent thus, Phil exclaimed, impatiently—

"Come on, Bob. We must not waste time here. There is much for us to do."

"It may not be time wasted," replied Bob, sharply. "But then, you are right, we need muchly to find some comfortable place in which to spend the night. Now, if we could only find a snug little cavern in the cliff somewhere—oh!"

A sharp cry escaped his lips and terminated the sentence. At that moment the boys had come to a little bend in the cliff walls which here described a semi-circle, leaving a sheltered little cove below, amply large enough for the anchorage of a good-sized ship.

But, in the bare face of the mighty wall of rock, full fifty feet above the sands below, and twenty feet below the level of the cliff, was an aperture large enough to accommodate the body of a man.

"Look at that, Phil !" cried Bob, enthusiastically. "There is just the place for our future home."

"Where ?" asked Phil, staring with all his eyes.

"Don't you see it ?"

"What, not that hole in the cliff ?"

"Even so."

"Humph ! You're crazy, Bob. How could we

ever get to it ? Again, how do you know that it is large enough ?"

"If it is not large enough we can make it larger," declared Bob, with confidence. "Perhaps you may have not noticed it, but the rock formation of that cliff is sandstone. With a good pickaxe, or any sharp steel instrument, I could fashion out a chamber in that soft sandstone in less time than you could possibly imagine."

"Well, that beats me !" cried Phil, at once catching on to the idea. "What a head you have got, Bob !"

"You can readily see what an advantageous place of residence it would be for us. Should the island prove to be inhabited by natives, which is more than likely, they would be apt to make war upon us. In such a place of defence they could not harm us."

"Hurrah !" cried Phil. "That is grand. If the stone works as easy as you say, there is no reason why we could not have chambers fashioned in there, and, if need be, another means of exit and entrance than over the face of the cliff."

"Exactly."

"But what do you propose to do first of all ?"

To his waist Bob had taken the precaution to tie a long rope. This he now proceeded to unwind and made reply—

"I want you to lower me over and let me enter the place ; I can then very soon learn how feasible the plan is."

"All right," agreed Phil.

With this they made a detour of the cliff-wall, and finally arrived at a point directly over the aperture.

Then, with the rope tightly secured to his waist, Bob allowed his chum to lower him over the cliff.

It was a hazardous proceeding, for a fall from that height must mean a frightful death ; but this did not deter Bob. Down over the face of the cliff he went, until finally he swung lightly into the aperture.

A cry of joy escaped him which reached Phil's listening ears.

The aperture proved but a narrow opening to a series of peculiar winding passages wrought by some strange freak of nature in the heart of the sandstone cliff.

Bob reappeared a few moments later and signalled Phil to draw him up. When he once more stood on the cliff wall, he said, joyfully—

"It seems a place designed for us. We need make no material change at present. It is all right to stop awhile in, in its present condition."

"Good !" cried Phil. "Let us go back after our effects, and move them right in here."

"First we must devise some sort of a better ladder to go in and out with."

For the present, however, the single rope was made to do the service of a ladder. It was given a turn securely about the trunk of a palm tree, and then the boys went back after their chests.

As it would save much laborious effort, the chests were carried along the beach to a place under the cliff house, whence they were hoisted up and into it.

Then the rope was drawn up and a temporary rope ladder was devised by utilising both ropes.

"They will do for a while," philosophised Bob. "But before they have time to get rotten we will try and make some sort of a rope with the fibres of

some of those odd looking vines which I see grow
all over the island."

With their effects safely moved into their cliff-
house abode, the boys felt quite secure and in
better spirits than they had been since the mutiny
on board the Pelican.

In the chests they had blankets, clothing, an
extra stock of ammunition, and their mechanical and
scientific instruments, with some of Bob's choice
books of science.

The blankets were utilised to make a good bed,
and nails were driven into the soft sand-stone walls,
and the rifles and instruments all hung up, so that
very quickly the cliff house began to look furnished
and cheerful.   A place was selected for a fire-place,
and Bob's ingenuity devised a species of plaster,
made from lime found upon the island and sand,
and with pieces of sandstone a chimney was devised
to carry the smoke out of the dwelling.

As Bob had predicted, the sandstone was easy to
work, and they conceived the idea of cutting a passage-
way, tending downward to the level of the beach,
as a means of exit in case the rope should fall.

But this was relegated to the future with many
other plans which the present exigencies could not
meet.

Fish was procured in the cave, a species of tooth-
some crab, and wild ducks were plentiful. The boys
were at no loss for the satisfying of their appetites.

So the first day passed and the boys slept in the
cliff house.

The next morning, Bob, with only the aid of a
chisel and mallet, cut a square window to the front
room of the abode looking seaward.

Even a rude lattice was rigged, and a telescope,

part of Bob's purchases, was placed in the window with which to scrutinise the sea line in the hopes of seeing a sail.

While Bob was laying out plans Phil was busy with the tools, fashioning the chambers into more convenient shape, so that in a few days the cliff house was an abode to be proud of.

Now that the first feeling of despair and loneliness had worn off, the boys became interested and even enamoured of their work.

There was a certain charm, a novelty in the fitting of their recluse abode which fired their young spirits with a sense of romance, and adventure most enjoyable.

The exploration of the island had been wisely left until the cliff house was made habitable and defensible, then one morning Bob made a proposal.

"We have our fortress constructed, Phil ; let us take a turn over the island now, and see what sort of a place we may have to spend our lives in."

"I am with you, Bob," cried Phil, picking up his rifle. "Come on !"

They left the cliff house, and struck out for the first time into the interior of the island.

To their surprise they saw from a height a region spread before them of wondrous beauty and luxuriance of vegetation.

Immense and impenetrable forests stretched for miles through mountain ranges, all over-shadowed by a mighty smoking volcano.

The young explorers penetrated as far as they could into the dense forest.

Thus far they had seen no sign of human life. Plenty of animals and birds abounded, from the chattering monkey to the striped leopard, which did not venture to attack the boys.

Presently the forest grew so thick that they could penetrate no further.

They came to a sluggish river, winding through dark and dense foliage, and here threw themselves down to rest and drink out of a clear spring.

"Well, if this is not a veritable Eden then I will give in," declared Bob, with enthusiasm.

But the words had barely left his lips, and Phil had no chance to make reply, when a chorus of guttural cries arose upon the air, and a score of dark forms emerged from the fastnesses of the forest and surrounded the boys.

Phil on the first impulse fired, and the foremost savage fell with affright, but he was not hurt; a moment later he was on his feet again.

CHAPTER XVII.

THE MAKOLOS.

HE situation in every sense of the word was thrilling and most undesirable.

The boys had been taken wholly by surprise. Both sprang up only to find a forest of spears aimed full at their breasts.

What could they do but surrender?

To have offered resistance would not only have been futile but the height of utter folly, There was no way to escape instant death.

A powerful, broad-chested band they were, and but for the smudging of their chocolate-hued countenances with greasy paint they would have been a very good-looking class of men.

These natives, while naked, save for the breech clout, were of a peculiar dark hue of skin, not negroes certainly.

For fully a minute the boys stood motionless, covered by the forest of spears.

While both felt sick and faint with the feeling that their fate was certainly sealed, particularly if these natives were cannibals, they never gave way to any outward sign of fear.

It was with a feeling of intense relief, however, that they saw the chief of the band with a guttural exclamation make a sign with his hand, and the spears were lowered and the natives fell back.

The chief was a tall, finely-formed man, with a not unkindly cast of features, and his manner now reassured the boys greatly.

He advanced from the throng and touching the palm of his hand to his brow, made a low, obsequious bow, which was not unlike the mode of salutation of an Arab Sheik.

At the same time he muttered some unintelligible jargon, and by signs gave his prisoners to understand that they need not fear harm.

Emboldened by this, Bob at once attempted to make sign talk with him.

This was not an easy task, but with every effort better success was accorded him, so that very quickly Bob got upon good terms with the native chief.

Bob found that they were inclined to be far from hostile and met the friendly manifestations more than half way.

The result was that in a few moments the fierce attitude was relaxed, the men cast down their spears and came forward with guttural grunts of approval. They sat down in various attitudes in a semi-circle, and the chief, whom his men addressed as Matafayo, resumed the sign talk.

"We come from beyond the great waters," Bob said, in sign talk. "Our people left us on the island. They were bad men. We want to make friends with you."

"The white men are welcome," was the chief's reply, in signs. "Many years have passed since white men came to us. They came once and made war upon our fathers."

Bob and Phil surmised that this must have been the visit of Captain Black and his pirate gang so many years ago, and shook their heads in disapproval.

"We are not that kind," intimated Bob. "We love peace."

"Then the white men are welcome. They must come to the village of the Makolos, and our young men and women will dance for them."

The boys hesitated before accepting this invitation, and Phil exchanged glances with Bob.

"Shall we go?"

"I don't know as we can get out of it."

"Well, it won't do any harm. We must make friends with these people."

So they signified their willingness, and Matafayo, the chief, who seemed much flattered, arose and with dignity motioned his warriors to precede them.

Then he accorded his visitors the honour of walking with them, and very soon coming into a well-beaten path in the forest, they made rapid progress, until suddenly the forest cleared and the blue sea was spread before them.

Both the boys gave an exclamation of surprise, for they had not fancied their position so near the sea, and Matafayo explained that here an arm of the ocean extended into the island, affording a smooth bay, upon the shores of which the village of the Makolos was situated.

They were even now in sight of the village, when a thrilling incident occurred.

A sort of deep jungle lay before them, and in skirting this a loud cry of terror suddenly escaped the warriors in front, and they scattered right and left. Chief Matafayo came to an instant halt, and sprang on one side into a small cave. All was done in the twinkling of an eye.

The boys heard a hoarse, snarling growl and saw a long, striped body shoot out of the jungle and plunge into the cave.

It had scattered the warriors, and seemed to have singled out the chief, for it sprang upon him with all the fury of the man-eater.

The tiger is an animal more to be dreaded than the lion, as it is more crafty, more deadly, and the inveterate foe of man, whom it is prone to hunt.

Matafayo had no time to make defence, and was crushed to the ground, the animal's jaws crunching through the bones of his shoulder.

It was a terrible moment.

With the form of his victim suspended in his powerful jaws the tiger stood for a moment, with head erect and growling savagely.

Poor Matafayo was wonderfully calm and plucky, however, and as he hung there helpless with the consciousness that his fate was sealed, he spoke reassuring words to his warriors.

The two boys, Bob and Phil, were horrified. But only for a moment were they inactive.

"Heavens! he is lost!" gasped Bob.

"Not if I can save him!" replied the plucky Phil.

Then he began edging his way rapidly around to the right. This brought the tiger's left shoulder exposed to view.

Crack!

The rifle spoke sharply and with most deadly effect.

The tiger leaped in the air with a wild howl and dropped his victim. He lashed his tail furiously and made a savage bound towards Phil.

But Phil was prepared for him, and fired straight into his chest.

The terrible beast made one plunge and then rolled in a struggling heap upon the ground. In two minutes he was lifeless.

The result was wonderful to witness.

Matafayo was just able to stagger to his feet and the natives came up slowly, and with apparent awe, gazing at the wonderful "fire-sticks" in the hands of the preservers.

In spite of the recent seriousness of the situation the boys laughed.

"I guess they never saw a gun before, Phil," remarked Bob.

"I should say not."

But the boys spoke reassuringly, and the superstitious Makolos advanced, and gave attention to their wounded chief.

It was found that Matafayo's wounds, while painful, were not apt to prove serious, and he was enabled to have them bound up with some pieces of linen and liniment which the boys had.

Then some of the Makolos fell to skinning the tiger, while the others crowded about the boys, gazing with wonder at the deadly guns.

Matafayo was especially curious, and, forgetting his wounds, literally beseiged the boys with questions.

"What makes it blaze?" he asked, in sign talk. "Where does the fire come from?"

Bob had some difficulty in explaining to him the explosive properties of the rifle cartridge.

But the native chief could not get through his brain the philosophy of the explosion when the hammer struck the cap.

He regarded the deadly cartridges almost reverently, and when Phil cut one of the bullets from the tiger's flesh in the region of the heart, he took it and placed it in his bosom.

"It will vanquish my enemies," he said. "It is sacred."

All of the natives regarded the boy owners of the wonderful firesticks with awe and an idea finally struck Bob.

"Would you like to see the gun go off?" he asked the chief.

Matafayo nodded his head eagerly.

Bob placed his handkerchief upon a distant limb of a tree. Then, measuring off a certain number of paces, he called the attention of the natives to his actions.

"You see I put this in here," he said, placing the cartridge in the breech. "Then I draw this back," drawing back the hammer. "Then I pull the trigger."

He suited the action to the word and fired. The handkerchief was seen to move and one of the natives brought it, showing a bullet-hole clean through it.

At the explosion the natives threw themselves on the ground in fear. But they gradually recovered from this.

Next Bob brought down a hawk which sat upon the high limb of a tree.

The natives ran and picked up the bird with wonderment, showing it's broken wing.

Then one of them placed his shield in the branches of a tree as a target, and Bob fired a bullet through it.

Matafayo expressed in signs his opinion that their shields would hardly be adequate defence against the firesticks. Bob and Phil agreed with him.

Then an idea occurred to Phil.

"Wouldn't you like to try it?" he said in signs to Matafayo.

The chief shook his head sadly, and indicated his wounded shoulder. But with an authoritative wave of his hand he commanded one of his men to come forward.

The fellow came trembling, but Bob partly re-assured him so that he held the gun to his shoulder quite steadily.

Then by Bob's direction he pulled the trigger. The result was too comical for anything.

With the explosion of the rifle the startled native dropped it and turned several back somersaults with the rapidity of lightning.

Then he ran for the village as fast as he could go, and did not again show up.

The chief laughed until his sides ached, as did Bob and Phil.

Then Matafayo commanded the shield to be brought to him.

But the last shot had went wide.

No bullet-hole was in it.

The chief's face was grave, and he could not seem to understand Bob's and Phil's explanation that the aim was not good.

He shook his head soberly, and in signs made the confident assertion that the white boys were possessed of the magic charm which enabled them to kill with the fire-sticks.

It being inadvisable to argue the point, and the tiger now being skinned, they started for the Makolo village, a collection of bamboo huts.

As they drew near a number of the natives came running out to meet them, and a sudden exclamation escaped Phil's lips as he clutched Bob's arm.

"As I live," he cried, "one of them is a white man like ourselves, Bob! What can he be doing here?"

There was no mistaking the fact. One of the advancing party was a white; though, save for an old pair of white duck trousers, he was as naked as the natives.

His beard grew down upon his chest and his hair over his shoulders.

His face was patrician its mould, though he was a man past the prime of life, and the boys could see that he was visibly affected at sight of them.

It required but a few moments to cover the intervening distance, and the white exile, for such he was, lifted his hands and rushed forward to embrace the boy maroons with a wild cry of joy.

"Heaven be thanked !" he cried. "Once more I behold people of my own nation. Oh ! say that you have come to take me away after my twenty years of this exiled life. Where is your ship ?"

"My good sir," said Bob, in tones of sadness, " I am sorry to visit disappointment upon you. But we are exiles upon this island fully as much as you."

The castaway's face fell for a moment, but quickly brightened.

"At least I can thank Heaven for his kindness in sending fellow beings of my own colour to me. Oh ! Mida will be overjoyed." Then, seeing a look of enquiry in Bob's eyes, he rejoined— "Mida is my daughter. When our ship sunk in mid-ocean, twenty years ago, she was but a child in my arms. For days we drifted about in an open boat, and by chance came across this island. These native people have been kind to us, and we have not been unhappy with them. Indeed, they have made me a chief amongst them. But where was your ship wrecked ?"

"Ah ! We were not cast away," replied Sam.

"Not cast away ?"

"No. We were put ashore."

"Good Heavens !" gasped the white chief. "How horrible ! Who could have been so cruel as to impose that fate upon you ?"

Bob and Phil briefly narrated the story of their adventures. Albert Cameron, which was the castaway's name, listened with deepest interest.

When they had finished, he said—

"You will hardly need your house in the cliff. These people are friendly, and you shall come and live with us. While you have my sympathy in your cruel fate, I am nevertheless selfish enough to feel joy that you are marooned upon this island. It is like a ray of sunlight across my life."

Both Phil and Bob were favourably impressed with Albert Cameron. They walked on now toward the village.

As they did so a young girl came out of one of the huts, and both Phil and Bob thought they had never seen such rare beauty as hers in all their lives.

She came timidly, bashfully, and was introduced by Mr. Cameron as his daughter Mida.

After an interchange of remarks, Mr. Cameron insisted on the boys coming into his hut to partake of dinner.

Matafayo, on the other hand, had invited them to his palace, but upon Mr. Cameron's explaining matters he was quite contented to accept an invitation to be present at the white chief's dinner.

Quite a sensation was created in the village by the arrival of the white boys.

The entire village turned out *en masse*, and thronged about the white chief's hut.

King Matafayo took advantage of this to call for a dance of the young men and women, and it was given in a manner at once picturesque and fantastic.

The boys witnessed it with interest, and then went in to partake of the meal arranged by Mida's deft hands.

After the dinner was over all sat down outside the hut and engaged in conversation.

The boys were more recently from the civilised world, so that they were enabled to give Mr Cameron a great deal of news.

The white chief listened with interest and asked numberless questions.

But at length it became the turn of the visitors, and Bob enquired—

"Are there other islands adjoining this one, Mr. Cameron?"

"Oh! yes," was the reply. "Half a score, at various distances. The nearest is but ten miles to the westward."

"Are they inhabited?"

"Yes."

"By the same class of people?"

"No," replied Mr. Cameron. "We have been fortunate in getting in with a very fine class of natives. Most of these islanders, if not cannibals, are at least bloodthirsty and treacherous."

"Indeed! Do they ever visit this island?"

"On rare occasions. Only two years ago we had a hard battle with three hundred cannibals just off the point there. We lost a hundred men but we defeated them."

"They have not come back since?"

"No."

"But do you not fear another visit?" asked Bob, with interest.

"We are prepared for it, but they may never come again. They come in huge war canoes."

"Another question," said Bob. "Can you tell me anything about the nine skeletons chained upon the cliff yonder?"

"What! Have you seen that already?" exclaimed Mr. Cameron, in surprise. "The natives never visit there. A superstitious fear keeps them away. Oh! yes, that is the handiwork of old Captain Black, the pirate. You have heard of him?"

"Yes," assented Bob and Phil in one breath.

" But would it not seem to you that at one time this was the pirate's rendezvous ?"

" I have no doubt of it."

" In that case is it unreasonable to suppose that there is a treasure buried on this island somewhere ?"

" It is quite reasonable," assented Mr. Cameron.

" Did you ever look for it ?"

" No. What would its discovery avail me? I would rather sight a ship and get off the island. Gold is below par here."

" Then you have little hopes of ever seeing home again ?"

" I have had so little belief that I should that I have in many ways conformed to the native mode of life. On the other hand, I have done much to try to civilise them."

" Good !" exclaimed Bob, with flashing eyes. " They are a very fine-looking, intelligent race for an uncivilised people, Mr. Cameron."

" Yes, they are."

" It would not be difficult to teach them the arts."

" I believe you."

" Why !" exclaimed Bob, enthusiastically, " I believe it would be possible in a lifetime to build up a small kingdom right here on this island. With a knowledge of the arts, how these people would progress !"

" You are right, but, alas ! I am not qualified to teach them. My knowledge of physics or mechanics is limited."

Bob said no more at the moment. But he was quite full with the idea from that time.

A strange, seemingly improbable dream had found shape in his brain, and he would not be satisfied until it had been executed.

"It can be done," he mused to himself. "These people can be taught the art of mining, of pottery, of making iron, and of tilling the ground, and building substantial houses. Ah! to found such an empire here I might forswear my native land."

Bob never did things by halves. At an opportune moment he separated from the others and walked down to the shore.

The site was a grand one for a small city. Here was a harbour capable of sheltering hundreds of ships.

It was a favourable spot to build wharves, and he already fancied a traffic with the great nations of the world in spices, in indigo, in fruits, minerals, and the many products of the wonderful isle.

Indeed, he waxed so enthusiastic over the subject that he fell to pacing up and down the shore, talking aloud to himself.

"At least we could open traffic with the natives of other islands about here, and if they are warlike we will conquer them. Gunpowder can easily be manufactured here, and with my knowledge of mining—oh!"

"Your pardon, Mr. Bob," said a musical voice—indeed, like the tinkling of silvery bells—at his elbow. "I am very sorry to have disturbed your meditations. This is my hour for exercise upon the water in my canoe."

"Miss Cameron!" exclaimed Bob, gallantly; "allow me to assist you."

And Bob assisted the young girl to place the light canoe in the water.

One moment she poised lightly in the feather-like craft upon the swell and smiled bewitchingly at Bob.

"You see I am a water-sprite!" she cried, with a merry laugh. "Oh! you need not look so fearful. If it tips over I can swim ashore."

"I must certainly compliment you on your skill," cried Bob, lifting his hat. "You are a very graceful canoeist, Miss Cameron."

Young ladies had rarely if ever made an impression upon the prosaic young fellow, but certainly Miss Mida Cameron had made a deep and lasting one.

He still stood watching the light canoe and its graceful occupant glide like a feather across the gleaming waters of the bay, when a rippling laugh in his ear called him back to his senses.

Phil and Mr. Cameron, with Matafayo and several of the natives, had come down to the shore.

"Well, Bob," cried Mr. Cameron, heartily. "Thinking of the future metropolis, eh? Ah! I am afraid the obstacles to your enterprise are many and great."

"Not so great but that they can be overcome," replied Bob, confidently.

"What is this?" asked Phil. "Got a new idea, Bob?"

"Yes, he is designing a great kingdom, to excel any other in the world, upon this productive island," said Mr. Cameron.

"Wonderful!" cried Phil, with youthful confidence leaping at the idea. "Why not carry it out, Bob?"

"At least we can make it our diversion while we are obliged to remain here," said Bob, confidently.

"Perhaps we may succeed so well that we will never want to leave the island."

"Good!" cried Phil, enthusiastically. "I will do my part, Bob. At least I can teach these chaps how to build houses and saw out lumber, or hew it out, if we have no saw-mill."

"And while you are doing that," declared Bob, "I will engage to mine and smelt the iron ore with which to manufacture the necessary tools."

CHAPTER XVIII.

LOST.

A FEW days later the two boys, with Mida and a faithful attendant of the black king, named Hyjah, went on a fishing excursion in a canoe.

When three miles from the island a sudden storm of wind came upon them, and despite the exertion of the natives they were blown away towards an island about ten miles distant.

Hyjah said it was inhabited by a tribe of their deadly enemies—the Bokaris—and most strenuous exertions were made to keep off the coast.

But the storm continuing they were obliged to land to escape drowning, and having drawn the canoe up on shore and hidden it they resolved to take refuge for a while on the side of a mountain which sloped down to the sea.

Hyjah said it was the safest thing they could do, as the Bokaris were always prowling round the coast of the island on the look out for foes who very often assailed them.

The shape of the mountain was peculiar, and Hyjah told the boys that it very often " spoke fire."

Just then lightning was playing round its summit, and the roll of thunder fell upon their ears.

They had just begun the ascent when a wild whoop was heard, and a host of the Bokaris burst out of a wood on the right, cutting off their retreat from the shore.

Perforce they had to flee up the mountain.

About a quarter of a mile intervened between them and their foes, and they looked to reach some safe hiding-place ; but suddenly a new peril assailed them.

The earth shook, and a tremendous black cloud uprose from the crown of the mountain. In several places huge cracks appeared.

And one of these not far from them poured out a stream of lava.

The mountain was again awake and speaking fire.

An awful darkness spread across the sky, relieved, however, by the almost incessant lightning. With such venturous and savage foes in pursuit their peril was indeed great.

Death in its most hideous, awful form impended over our friends, and only a seeming miracle saved them.

To retreat before the oncoming lava would have been madness. To go to the right or left there was no time, for its course was wide.

But Bob had observed a dark spot in the side of the mountain but a few feet above his position.

The reflected glare of light now revealed to his startled gaze the yawning mouth of a cavern.

In an instant he dragged Mida toward it, crying—

"Come quickly. For our lives. It is a cave, and here is safety for us."

At the same moment Phil and Hyjah saw the cavern.

It did not take them hardly an instant of time to reach it. Mida was fairly carried by the boys.

Into the cavern for a distance of ten feet they went and then sank down from sheer exhaustion.

They were saved.

Just by a hair's-breadth, though.

The mighty volume of lava went pouring down the mountain over the mouth of the cavern. It made the air stifling within, but luckily its volume was not permanent.

Bob sat up and wiped the perspiration from his face.

"That was the most narrow escape I ever had," he declared. "I wouldn't care to go through it again."

"Nor I," cried Phil.

As for Hyjah, he made rantic gestures.

Mida raised herself upon her elbow and said—

"Oh! I cannot thank you enough for all you have risked and done for me. I shall never forget it."

"We are only too happy to serve you," said Bob, gallantly.

"We would not have been men not to have attempted your rescue," rejoined Phil.

"You are heroes in my eyes," cried the young girl with tearful eyes. "Oh! if we escape from here and reach our island home safely, my father will not fail to reward you, at least with his undying gratitude. You have mine until death."

"We hope to reach our island-home safely," said Bob, hopefully. "So far Providence has guided us."

Phil arose and went to the mouth of the cave.

The flow of lava had ceased now, but the ground was unfit to walk on, and to leave the cavern was an impossibility.

There was no alternative but to spend the night in the place; so our friends made themselves as comfortable as possible.

Gradually as the night wore on the mighty trembling of the mountain ceased and the air became cooler. When daylight came the volcano only emitted flame and smoke at intervals.

But what a scene was spread below. Such ruin and desolation our friends had never seen before; the fertile valley had been transformed by the fire fiend into a vale of utter devastation.

But it was easy to leave the cavern now. The masses of lava had cooled, and Bob, assisting Mida, led the way down the mountain.

The boy maroons were well aware that it was necessary to proceed with the greatest caution.

It was more than likely that the Bokaris would be on the lookout for them. Therefore, they kept as much as possible behind obstructions, such as rocks and mounds, until the valley was reached.

Here Hyjah was allowed to go ahead and reconnoitre.

He returned very soon with the joyful intelligence

that the coast was clear, so far as the Bokaris were concerned.

But a wide stream, fully one hundred feet broad, of molten lava intervened between them and a direct line to the sea coast.

This stream of lava might extend into the valley for a mile or more. To cross it was quite impossible.

This intelligence rather put a damper upon the spirits of all. It was a set-back not anticipated.

There were just two ways to overcome the difficulty.

One was to remain where they were until the stream of lava cooled, which might be a whole day yet, or endeavour to go around it. Neither of these plans was pleasant to contemplate.

It was more than likely that the Bokaris would return as soon as the danger from the eruption was past. To remain would be to risk encountering them.

To attempt to go around the stream of lava was not easy. This might even lead them into the very camp of the enemy.

Bob looked blankly at Phil.

"What are we going to do?"

That was a puzzler.

"Can we not bridge the stream in some way?" asked Phil.

"No," replied Bob, positively. "What material have we? Rock even would be no barrier."

This was true. It was a most unpleasant situation.

However, they kept on until the bank of the lava stream was reached. It was seen at a glance how impossible it was to cross it.

They stood disconsolately upon the bank of the fiery stream and waited, hoping that it would abate its volume.

But there was a mighty reservoir of the molten stuff in the crater of the volcano.

Had it occurred to the boys to go up the mountain-side at that moment they would have found an easy means of crossing.

At a certain point the stream narrowed to a width of scarcely three feet between high jutting rocks.

This they were destined to discover later.

They remained some time at this point vainly cogitating upon some means of crossing the lava stream when a warning cry broke from Hyjah's lips.

The others turned and were rewarded with a startling sight.

Directly up the valley towards them on the run were advancing a band of the Bokaris.

They were yelling wildly, having caught sight of our adventurers. It was a thrilling moment.

In front was the stream of lava. Behind were the deadly foe. What was to be done?

The outlook might well have caused stouter hearts to quail.

But Bob started up the mountain for the cover of some rocks above. He picked up his elephant rifle and inserted an explosive shell.

"I'll teach them a lesson," he muttered, as he took aim.

Straight into the horde he fired. The explosive bullet, being of the kind used in India to kill elephants and the hippopotamus, struck one of the islanders and exploded.

"Hurrah!" cried Phil. "Give it to 'em, Bob."

Bob was rushing up the mountain-side and paused to fire again.

Phil and the others were just below. Just as Bob fired a strange thing happened.

The ground gave way underneath him, and in a twinkling he vanished from sight.

Phil and the others halted aghast. Then Phil sprang forward and gazed down into the hole.

As he did so a sulphurous jet of steam and smoke came up and filled the orifice. This settled all doubt.

"Oh! Heaven," cried Phil in an abandon of grief. "Bob is lost. He has gone to his death.

CHAPTER XIX.

BACK AGAIN.

HORROR, blended with anguish, was predominant in their souls as our adventurers realised the fact that Bob was gone beyond any possibility of rescue.

The outcome of smoke and steam from the orifices must preclude any other supposition but that he was ere this consumed by fire, perhaps thousands of feet below in the crater of the volcano.

For the moment they forgot the Bokaris, and

Phil was wringing his hands in an insane manner when Hyjah clutched his arm.

Then the boy came to his senses, and in that swift instant realised the folly of sacrificing his own life as well as the lives of the others.

He turned and offered Mida his arm.

"We will fight to the end," he muttered, grimly.

Phil started for the cover of the rocks above. As it was reached a great cry of joy escaped his lips. He saw that here it was possible to cross the lava current.

"Why did we not see this before?" he cried. "We can now escape."

Hyjah took one of Mida's arms and Phil the other. They crossed the river of lava, and, fairly carrying the young girl, sped down the mountain.

The Bokaris reached the lava stream, and it was some time before they discovered the place of crossing.

By that time our friends had reached the cover of the dense woods. Phil paused only to fire a parting shot, and then they made a bee-line for the coast. They soon came out upon the sandy beach. Mida bore up bravely.

The wreck of the Pelican was passed again, and finally the spot was reached where they had left the canoe.

It was but a moment's work to shove it out and embark. Phil trimmed the sail, and they went scudding out to sea before a fine breeze.

But as they made an offing from the island the shore became thronged with islanders. They had escaped none too soon.

Fortunately the Bokaris had no canoes at that point, so they could not offer pursuit.

Before an hour the Bokari Island had sunk out of sight upon the horizon. At nightfall their own island was sighted, and they beat in the little bay on whose shores was the Makolo village.

Their appearance was the signal for wild demonstrations on the part of the Makolo warriors. All the people came rushing down to the shore, and drums were beaten.

Mida stepped ashore, to be clasped in her frantic father's arms. It was a meeting to draw tears from an image of stone.

Matafayo stood near and greeted the brave Hyjah with an approving smile. Mr. Cameron turned from Mida and seized Phil in his arms.

"It is to you two brave boys that I owe all," he cried wildly. "But—your companion—Bob, where is he?"

One swift, enquiring glance the white chief of the Makolos gave Phil, then the colour fled from his face.

"Mercy !" he gasped, "you don't mean that harm has come to him?"

"Bob—is—dead," said Phil, in a choking voice, then flung himself upon the sands in an ecstasy of grief. Mr. Cameron was quite overcome.

Phil Farren felt the loss of his chum keenly, and would not be comforted that night. Even Mida's soothing tones had but a transient effect upon him.

The next day, however, he was calmer and went about his duties in a methodical manner.

"Bob was as dear as a brother to me," he said, sincerely. "We had planned to accomplish so much, and now I am left to do it alone."

But he was firmly resolved to carry out those

plans so fondly cherished by Bob, to found a beautiful city upon the island and attempt the civilisation of the Makolos.

He imparted all this to Mida and Mr. Cameron, and they entered into the project with heart and soul.

"We will make the best of our loss," said Mr. Cameron, bravely. "I have some knowledge of the smelting and working of iron ore."

"Have you?" cried Phil, eagerly.

"Yes."

"There are fine deposits of minerals on the islands."

"Indeed, there is a supply of almost everything we need. I am with you, my boy. You can go to work on your lumbering and the teaching of your men how to handle the tools—"

"Ah!" exclaimed Phil, ruefully. "There is the rub. My tools are but few in number."

"Do as well as you can," cried Mr. Cameorn. "I will do my part. My first move will be to put a gang of men at work in a clay bank not far from here, making brick—"

"You understand the process?"

"Yes."

"Hurrah! We shall have chimneys for our houses and a smelting furnace and chimney. Let us to work."

Phil became in a measure oblivious of his sorrow in the new project.

Matafayo was consulted and readily furnished a quota of men, overseeing them personally. The Makolos were very intelligent and apt.

Mida was not without her department. She had decided to found a school and teach the little Makolos the English language as well as their own, and the rudiments of reading and writing.

Phil went to the cliff house, which he and Bob had constructed, and brought away his tools.

There were axes and saws and chisels in plenty for a small gang. But the minor and equally important tools, such as planes and shaving implements, were few in number.

First of all it was necessary to teach his inexperienced workmen how to fell a tree and lop the branches.

This art was easily acquired.

Then came the laborious work of hewing and sawing, and in the latter Phil was greatly helped by a long two-handed saw, which, fortunately, he possessed.

The natives watched his operations and accepted his directions with much awe though deep interest.

They were clamorous for an opportunity to learn the new arts, and so Phil found that it was not necessary to drive them to their woork.

Thus the days passed, the men going out every day to their work just as in civilised countries.

The little island village was the scene of great activity and bustle.

Having hewn the timbers, Phil proceeded to frame a small house.

Mr. Cameron had drawn rocks and laid a foundation, and already had manufactured sun-dried bricks for the chimney.

Phil finally completed the frame of the new house, and then came the ceremony of raising it upon the fine stone foundation.

It was a gala day in the Makolo village when in exactly two weeks from the date of beginning the first house in the city was given tangible shape by raising the frame.

But at this juncture Phil was brought to a stand-still.

Wooden pins would unite the sills and frame, but nails were needed for the floors and sheathing.

To make something from nothing is a feat rarely undertaken successfully. Yet this was what our colonists, if such a term be proper, practically did.

While Phil had been raising the frame of the house Mr. Cameron had not been idle.

He had, with a quantity of peculiar clay, of which the island boasted, actually succeeded in fashioning a furnace and retort, perhaps of rude fashion, yet effective.

Coal was dug and a large furnace fire made.

Then the iron was mined, and by the usual process reduced to a pig state.

At first a heap of this pig served for an anvil, and with an improvised hammer Mr. Cameron actually beat out a fair quantity of wrought iron nails for the house.

A great step towards civilising the Makolos had been made.

To teach them comprehensively the art of developing iron ore was to place in their hands a most valuable adjunct for the overcoming of all obstacles.

It may be truly said that iron is the foundation of the civilised world.

Without it other minerals could not be fitly developed. Woods could not be satisfactorily worked, and weapons of war would be funny affairs.

One month witnessed a great stride for the Makolos. Every one of them, men, women, and children, were interested and learned with surprising rapidity.

They observed wonderingly the shape and architecture of the new building.

Phil had sawed out boards not without great labour, and even shingle for the roof.

The result was that in the short space of six weeks the structure was finished.

Lime was found in abundance, and plaster was made with the hair of goats found on the island.

There were four rooms in the house and one of them was accorded Matafayo, who straightway became the proudest man on the island.

All this accomplished, Phil now changed his plans.

He did not keep on building houses for the present. Other matters of far more importance were suggested to him.

The Makolos were essentially a peace-loving people

Their enemies, the Bokaris, were more than a match for them. Phil foresaw what a calamity it would be should a raid be made upon the island.

He conveyed his fears to Matafayo, who shared them.

Accordingly, Phil acted upon the old-time principle, " In time of peace prepare for war," and at once set a gang of men at work beating iron spear-heads out of the crude iron, as well as arrow tips, and other weapons which would be superior to those used by the Bokaris.

Mr. Cameron, with his clay and brick workers, now began work upon an extensive stone fort over the cliff, and where the people could seek safety and hold the enemy at bay.

Of course all this work was primitive, yet it was progressive, and gave promise of better things in the future.

Phil dreamed of a day when gunpowder and rifles would be manufactured on the island and the iron horse would make a circuit of its shores.

But he set this down as only the possible outcome of future years.

He even outlined the wide avenues and streets of the city, and made a plan of large wharves, where schooners would be moored to take on their cargo of valuable spices and dye stuffs, which would make of the Makolo island a miniature empire.

All this was extremely pleasant and enjoyable to the ambitious lad, and but for the gnawing sorrow for Bob's fate he would have been extremely happy.

Two months passed away like a brief dream, and Phil proceeded to carry out a plan which he had formed of a prospecting tour into the interior of the island.

With only one companion, the faithful Hyjah, he set out. It was his plan to search for minerals, but he never dreamed of the surprise in store for him. It will be remembered that when the boys first set foot upon the island they had observed what seemed like the smoke of a volcano in the interior. Phil had quite forgotten this fact, though it was now suddenly recalled to him, when, upon mounting an eminence, he caught sight of the smoking mountain, not five miles distant.

Phil had mastered a smattering of the Makolo

tongue, so that with the aid of signs he was enabled to talk with Hyjah quite intelligibly.

"Is the volcano ever very active?" he managed to ask.

Hyjah nodded his head eagerly, and manifested by signs the fact that eruptions were of frequent occurrence, when the destructive ashes and cinders nigh ruined the vegetation of the whole island.

For the first time Phil's plans seemed to receive a set-back. Of course, it would be vastly better to found an empire such as he had conceived upon stable ground.

"But, then," he mused, "it may not break out again for years, and may in time become extinct."

He dismissed the matter from his mind, and began to make an examination of the ledges which he now found himself amongst.

With Hyjah he wandered about over vast piles of volcanic rocks, and finally arrived at the conclusion that he was in the wrong part of the island for minerals, when he made an astounding discovery.

Close by the base of a high cliff they came upon a startling sight. Hyjah gave a sharp cry and sprang forward.

Upon the rock-strewn ground were two bleached human skeletons. They were in an attitude which showed a death struggle.

The fleshless fingers of one clutched what was once the throat of the other.

While a knife, rusted and crumbling with decay, was inserted between the ribs of one skeleton.

The story was told as plainly as if with words.

Years previously two men, deadly enemies, had here fought to the death. Both had perished, and these were their remains.

CHAPTER XX.

THE TIGER—THE BOKARI ATTACK.

THE story had a frightful moral. But what interested Phil and his native companion most was the fact that just at the back of the skeletons was the opening of a small cave.

It could not be seen how far into the rock it extended.

In the mouth of the cave was a heavy iron-bound chest.

The ancient covering of leather had long since crumbled away, and the oak was fast becoming honey-combed with the effects of Time.

In fact, as Phil advanced and touched it with his foot it fell apart, and a strange thing happened.

Out upon the rocky floor of the cave was spread broadcast a heap of gold coins.

They were heavy Spanish doubloons, and almost as bright as the day they came from the mint.

Phil uttered a cry, and kneeling down, picked up a handful of them.

"What a treasure!" he cried, excitedly. "Beautiful gold! Ah! but here's a sequel. Those unfortunate men no doubt came to their miserable end on account of it. I feel as if it were almost accursed."

He flung the gold pieces down, and then examined the skeletons.

First he removed the knife from the ribs of the uppermost one, and examined it closely.

He was rewarded by finding upon it an inscription in Spanish—

"The property of Captain Black."

"Captain Black, the pirate!" he cried. "No doubt this cave was the hiding-place of his ill-gotten treasure. Come on, Hyjah! Here is an adventure for us, for, as sure as my name is Phil, I mean to know what is in there. Let us explore the cave."

Phil acted wholly upon impulse in entering the cave with Hyjah at his elbow.

The discovery that one of the skeletons was undoubtedly that of Captain Black, the famous pirate, had fired his interest and excited his curiosity. Such a thing as danger had not occurred to him.

But that there was danger in entering the cave was quickly proved. A pair of fiery eyes, and a low, ominous growl caused Phil to come to a halt.

Some wild animal was in the place. For an instant Phil was disposed to beat a quick retreat. Then he overcame this feeling, and threw his rifle to his shoulder.

Crack!

The report reverberated like thunder into the cavern depths. Phil had fired directly between the flashing eyes. Had he taken second thought he would not have not done this.

The animal was a huge tiger, of the man-eating species, and the bullet, though striking true to the mark, glanced off his thick skull like a drop of water from a duck's back.

The next instant a powerful cat-like form descended upon Phil like an avalanche, and he was borne to the floor like a puppet. Only one thing saved his life.

It being dark in the place the beast might have miscalculated his spring, for certain it was that his momentum carried him far over his victim's body.

The tiger rolled over upon the stone floor, but was quickly upon its feet. Phil had fallen into a sort of crevice in the rocky floor, and was for a moment out of the animal's sight.

One blow of those mighty paws, one grip of the prodigious jaws, and the boy's life would have been ended.

Presently the tiger looked about for his victim , and, seeing Hyjah, sprang for him.

The plucky Makolo was armed with a long, sharp-pointed javelin.

Instinctively he thrust this before him.

The weapon was broken like a reed, and Hyjah was dashed to the floor, but by some miraculous chance the javelin point entered the eye of the tiger, and there it remained.

Deprived partly of his vision, and frantic with pain, the animal for a moment ignored his foe and placed both paws over his head, grovelling upon the stone floor and snarling like a demon.

Phil was upon his feet by this time, and saw his opportunity.

Without an instant's hesitation he rushed upon the tiger, and, thrusting the muzzle of his repeating rifle close against the tiger's shoulder, fired. The ball passed through the animal's heart. With a convulsive leap in the air and several gasping cries the monster lay quivering in death.

It was a terrific combat and a narrow escape for our friends.

Now that the peril was over Phil trembled like an aspen leaf.

Hyjah was weak and terrified, and well he might have been, for it was a close shave.

"I wouldn't care to take the chances over

again," declared Phil. "We are no match for such a big fellow as this."

"Take care," said Hyjah, apprehensively, in sign talk. "He may have a mate hereabouts."

But a few moments examination of the cavern disproved this fear.

"I will take his skin home for Mida," Phil decided. "But first let us see what sort of a stronghold Captain Black has here."

The cavern did not penetrate into the solid rock more than fifty feet.

There were three distinctive chambers, one of these being divided by masonry.

There were heaps of mouldering blankets, coats, and knee-breeches—clothes after the pattern of a century previous.

Old flint lock carbines, with cutlasses, and dirks of ancient make, were piled in one corner, while several kegs of gunpowder, which Phil found were in good condition, were also found in the cave.

"Hurrah!" he cried. "This is the most valuable discovery of all. We need not now go short of ammunition."

There were also some articles of furniture, tables, chairs, and seamen's chests thrown about.

In one corner the tigress had made her nest and raised her litter of young. The air was close and noisome, and Phil was finally glad to quit the place.

"This is quite a discovery," he reflected. "We need not now fear the attacks of the Bokaris. There are several hundred stands of small arms, which can be used by our people, as well as the cutlasses. Altogether we may now have a well equipped army. As soon as we can find a means of procuring saltpetre we shall manufacture our own gunpowder. So much for progress in the building up of our empire."

Phil was in a jubilant frame of mind, and on leaving the cavern he placed a few of the gold doubloons in his pocket.

"They are of little value to us here," he mused. "But if it should so happen that we ever return to civilisation, they will be of some use to us then."

The day was now drawing to a close, but Phil was not yet ready to return to the village.

In a deep ravine, some distance in the interior, he found unmistakable evidences of a rich deposit of iron ore. It was of a better quality than any yet discovered.

The vein seemed to run through the face of the cliff wall, but in examining it a well-nigh fatal accident happened.

Hyjah, flat upon his stomach, was peering over the edge of the cliff, when it crumbled beneath him.

Phil saw him going and sprang forward to save him.

But he was just too late. With an awful cry of terror Hyjah went over the verge.

It was a fall of five hundred feet to the depths below, and meant certain death.

There seemed nothing to save the unfortunate native.

"Oh ! Heaven," gasped Phil, with blanched face. "He is lost !"

But a seeming miracle saved him. Twenty feet down, on the scarp face of the precipice, there grew a solitary shrub. Hyjah fell directly into this and there lodged.

A wild cry of joy went up from Phil's lips.

"Hold fast, Hyjah!" he shouted. "I will save you!"

But the danger was not over yet by any means. Phil had no rope or other means of reaching his companion.

The shrub was not strong, and might at any moment give way and let the unfortunate fellow down to a horrible death.

It was an awful suspenseful moment. What was to be done? For a moment Phil was completely at a loss how to act.

So terrified was he that great beads of cold sweat came out upon his brow. Faithful Hyjah, terrified yet calm, clung to his perch.

"Hold fast, my brave fellow," Phil said, tersely. "I will save you or die in the attempt."

Phil was deadly in earnest. At that moment a happy idea occurred to him, and he acted upon it at once.

Long trailing vines covered the huge rock near. These were often used by the natives as ropes, they being pliable and strong.

In less time than it takes to tell it, Phil uprooted one of these and lowered it over the edge of the cliff.

Just in time, too, for the shrub to which Hyjah clung was already beginning to give away.

In a few seconds the nimble native was safe by Phil's side. The boy was so overjoyed that he could not resist giving Hyjah an embrace.

"We have had enough for one day," he declared excitedly. "Come, Hyjah, let us return home."

The native was more than willing, and they set out at once.

Phil was thinking of his good luck in finding the gunpowder, and picturing Mr. Cameron's surprise at the good news, when they came suddenly in sight of the Makalo town, and a great cry escaped Hyjah.

At the same moment Phil saw the cause of the native's terror.

The bay was crowded with native canoes, and a swarm of black warriors were being landed. It was the Bokari warriors, who had come to make an attack upon the Makolos.

A fearful, bloody battle was impending.

For a moment Phil was speechless with horror at sight of the Bokari warriors.

Then all the lion in his nature was aroused.

His eyes flashed, and his breast heaved with violent emotions.

"This is fearful work!" he cried. "They mean to annihilate us if they can. But they shall have a costly victory. Come, Hyjah, now is the time for action. There is war in full blast, and we must fight even to the death."

Hyjah gave the war-cry of the Makolos, and with Phil by his side started for the scene of action.

Phil loaded his repeater as he ran.

It seemed as if he would never reach the village.

The Bokaris had landed a large force, and were directing a murderous attack upon the Makolos.

The situation was critical.

Mr. Cameron was vainly endeavouring to organise the Makolos into a line of defence on one side of the town, and Matafayo was doing the same at the other side.

The Bokaris were making good their landing. In vain the Makolos tried to hold them back.

The cannibal king, in a mantle of tiger-skin, and with a huge shield and war-club, was ably directing the attack.

The Bokaris were fierce fighters.

But Danton, to Phil's utter amazement, was foremost in the attack.

He carried a long cutlass, or, rather, sword, and made sweeping blows, inciting the cannibals on with fierce cries.

The sensations experienced by Phil may well be imagined.

At that moment death held no terrors for him. He was so thoroughly wrought up that he would have faced a battery of guns without flinching.

Hyjah was by his side, and when they reached the Makolo village they met a terrified concourse of women and children.

Phil sprang forward and clasped Mida Cameron's hands in his.

The young girl was white and awestruck, but yet calm.

"Oh! I fear we are lost," she said, with blanched lips. "What will become of us all?"

"Courage!" cried Phil, bravely. "We will not yet yield. But you must not remain here. If the enemy should outflank us you would be wholly at their mercy."

"These women and children must have refuge," said Mida.

"And you?"

"Never mind me," replied the young girl, firmly. "I do not fear death. I prefer to remain here and assist the wounded."

"That will not do!" cried Phil. "You must all retreat to some safe place. Come here, Hyjah."

The young Makolo advanced and bowed low.

"You must take all these women and children to the cavern from which we have just come. Do you understand?"

The Makolo nodded in reply, and at once set about the performance of his task. Phil was obliged to argue with Mida, but finally induced her to go.

CHAPTER XXI.

A DESPERATE BATTLE.

AVING seen his instructions carried out, Phil now turned to the scene of battle.

The Makolos, under the cover of their houses, built by the ingenuity of the boy maroons, were bravely holding the foe at bay.

The air was filled with flying arrows and javelins.

Mr. Cameron was loading and firing with his rifle as rapidly as possible.

Every shot counted. But the Bokaris had come in great numbers, and fought recklessly, literally throwing their lives away in the battle.

The Makolos held their positions steadily, directed by the cool judgment of Mr. Cameron.

Phil called to mind the ammunition and weapons stored in Captain Black's cave, and the idea of a retreat to that spot was uppermost in his mind.

He passed through the line, heedless of the flying arrows, and reached Mr. Cameron's side.

Pale and determined, the white chief of the Makolos welcomed him joyfully.

"I am glad you have come," he said "This is a fight for our lives, Phil. If we lose, then our fate is settled."

"Yes," agreed Phil; "to fall into Bud Danton's hands now would mean death."

"Don't you think we had better make a stand here?"

"As long as possible."

"When we are driven from here—"

"I have a place to go to."

Mr. Cameron looked surprised.

"Where?"

"Have you a moment to spare?"

Fortunately there was a lull in the fighting just now, and Phil took advantage of it to detail to Mr. Cameron all the adventures which had befallen him in the past twelve hours. The island exile listened with great wonderment.

"And I have been all these years on this island and never discovered that cave yet," he exclaimed, with amazement. "This beats me."

"I think it is a great stroke of good luck."

"Certainly it is. Why, with those carbines, even if they are flint-locks, we can defeat a larger force than the Bokaris can bring, so long as their weapons consist only of bows and arrows."

"Yes, that is true."

"It will be, however, necessary to make a stand here as long as possible, to prevent the village falling into the hands of the enemy. If we are repulsed, then we can fall back upon the cave."

"Exactly."

A series of wild yells and a flight of arrows at this juncture announced that the Bokaris were returning to a fresh attack.

Mr. Cameron's voice went down the line like a trumpet call.

"Hold fast, every man!" he cried, in the Makolo tongue. "All depends on now. Drive them back once more, and victory is ours."

But Danton and the cannibal king had evidently decided to make this attack a decisive one, for the Bokaris came on like a shrieking pack of demons.

It seemed almost impossible to hold the Makolo line before such an attack.

They wavered, and seemed likely to break. Only the quick nerve and ready wit of Phil saved the day.

At the risk of his life he rushed in front of the wavering line, and with loud cries and daring example compelled them to reform.

Matafayo, the Makolo chief, came to Phil's aid, and the natives, thus reassured, made a mighty effort and turned the tide of battle. The Bokaris were driven back.

But it did not require a keen perception to see at a glance that a few more such attacks must surely break the line.

Blood-stained and damp with perspiration, Phil rejoined Mr. Cameron.

"Heaven!" he exclaimed, with pallid face. "Another such attack, I fear, would sweep our men away."

"It is a pity," exclaimed the island exile. "The Makolos are not well instructed in the art of war. If we had fifty good men—veterans, as it were—we could whip those dogs with ease."

"Fifty English sailors would annihilate them."

"Undoubtedly."

"But we haven't that material. However, we will make the best of it. If we break line—what then ?"

"We must not break," said Mr. Cameron, desperately, setting his teeth. "Once more they come, Phil. Now for life and liberty—all stand !"

The Bokaris were again forming to make a charge, which it seemed certain would sweep the Makolo line away.

It was a fearful, critical moment, and every man's heart was in his mouth. The meeting must decide the battle.

CHAPTER XXIII.

RETREAT TO THE CAVE.

GOOD general knows intuitively when his men are overmatched. It needed nothing more than this sense of intuition to convince Phil that theirs was a hopeless case.

But he was not the one to easily give up the strife.

As long as life lasted he would fight, and, after all, it was not a dishonourable way to meet death.

He compressed his lips firmly, and firing every cartridge in his repeater, rushed into the fight with clubbed rifle.

Of course the Makolos were in a measure inspired by his example, and for a time rallied.

But the stronger Bokaris came down like an avalanche.

They swarmed upon the breastworks erected by Phil's skill, rushed through the stake fence, battered their way into the houses, and drove the Makolos like sheep before them.

For a time it looked as if the battle would be nothing less than a wholesale massacre; but, finally, with a chosen number, Mr. Cameron and Phil held the foe at bay and covered the retreat.

The repeating rifles were responsible for this, for the Bokaris were loth to rush upon the muzzles of such death-dealing weapons.

Meanwhile Hyjah had returned from escorting the women and children to Captain Black's cave.

It was an opportune thing, for Phil set him at work organising a masterly retreat to the same place.

It gratified the boy maroon not a little to note that the majority of the Makolos were escaping unscathed, though fully one hundred of them lay dead in the village.

Slowly and in orderly fashion Mr. Cameron and his men fell back and joined Phil's force.

Then they reached the cover of the hillsides, and here the Bokaris, satisfied with their victory, came to a halt.

Night was coming on, and the great battle, which had ended in a defeat for the Makolos, was at an end.

Yet the consequences might have been worse, and Phil and Mr. Cameron congratulated themselves on their safe retreat.

In the cover of the hills it was easy to reform and recuperate exhausted energies.

The matter for regret was the loss of their first position, for it placed the village in the hands o the Bokaris, who would undoubtedly destroy it.

Phil saw all his plans of empire suddenly demolished. But this should only be temporary he told himself.

The Bokaris should yet be driven from the island, and victory perch upon the Makolo banner.

In this resolve he relied upon the store of ammunition in Captain Black's treasure cave.

Night settled down over the island calm and peaceful. A beautiful moon rode high in a placid sky, and the view seaward was like looking over the surface of a glistening mirror.

Phil and Mr. Cameron conferred upon the subject of withdrawing their outposts to the hills.

It seemed the better way, for the Bokaris would be almost sure to resume their attack on the following day.

At present they were holding high carnival in the village, celebrating their victory.

The withdrawal was effected safely and silently, and during the night Phil caused temporary breast-works to be erected upon a height which it would seem impossible for an enemy to scale.

Moreover, at the back of them was a large tract of rich, productive country, so that they need not fear starvation.

Their position now seemed invincible.

Phil found all the women and children huddled

in the cave. He enjoyed a few moments' conversation with Mida, and then gave his attention to the comfort of the others.

Substantial quarters were arranged for the women. The men could sleep out-of-doors anywhere, so no further thought was given to them that night.

But the next morning Phil was astir early, and had all the men sharp at work.

He invaded the innermost recesses of the cave, and brought forth all the antiquated carbines once used by the pirates.

These he caused to be thoroughly scoured and cleansed.

Nothing was heard of the Bokaris that day, they remaining quietly in the village.

But fresh canoe loads of reinforcements arrived, which was proof positive that they meant to carry the island. Phil compressed his lips firmly, and only muttered—

"We shall see. I think I have a surprise party for Bud Danton."

All the carbines, by Phil's direction, had been loaded and stacked in an open space on the cliff. Phil now directed Matafayo to summon his men and draw them up in line.

Not a few of the Makolo warriors understood the use of a gun. There were half a hundred in number, having been educated by Mr. Cameron.

These were at once given carbines and several rounds of ammunition. This made quite a bodyguard, and they were at once posted at different vulnerable points.

The others were then quickly instructed by Phil in the loading and firing of the carbines.

A target was set up, and each man was individually instructed how to load, aim, and fire.

The Makolos were an intelligent, apt class of people, and quickly caught on.

It was a coveted weapon for them, and the greatest enthusiasm prevailed.

Those who could skilfully load and use the new weapons strutted about with an amusing sense of superiority.

Several days were consumed in this manner, and in drilling and organising the Makolos.

All this while the Bokaris had been holding sacred feasts in the village. It was a fortunate thing for our friends that they had not followed up their attack.

Phil was much encouraged with the outlook now.

He hoped for really great results with the new weapons.

While the Makolos might not at first be great marksmen, their fire must necessarily be more destructive than that of arrows.

"We will defeat the enemy yet !" he cried, enthusiastically. "They shall be driven from our shores, or I miss my mark."

"I shall pray for success," said Mida, who had overheard the remark.

"I want to draw a bead on the pirate Danton," said Mr. Cameron, resolutely. "I will rid the earth of one monster. Once he is out of the way there will be one great disturbing element disposed of.

"Right you are !" cried Phil. "Whichever one of us sees him first will have the honour of putting a hole through his miserable carcase."

"Look out that he does not first draw a bead on you," admonished Mida.

At this moment Hyjah came up excitedly. The conversation just given was taking place on the morning of the fourth day since the defeat.

"They are coming!" cried Hyjah, excitedly, in the Makolo tongue. "And they must be one thousand in number. I never saw such an army of them."

At that moment a mighty column of smoke was seen to arise high in the air. It came from a point exactly over the village.

"They have fired the town," said Phil, with a sudden lump in his throat. "Our embryo metropolis will soon be in ashes, Mr. Cameron."

"Very well," declared the island exile, with a flash of resolution in his eyes. "We cannot help that, but we can plot for revenge."

Phil took up his repeater and inserted sixteen cartridges in it.

He was now ready for the fray which was close at hand.

CHAPTER XXV.

RUIN AND DESPAIR.

AND all this time, strange as it may seem, Bob, given up for lost, was alive. Let us, in as brief a manner as possible, tell what had become of him. When he fell through the opening, he dropped down at least ten feet, and then found himself rolling down a slope, apparently into the bowels of the earth.

He shouted and clutched the sides, endeavouring to stop his course, not thinking at the moment that it was his earthly salvation.

He was rolling down a natural sloping shaft

into pure air. Above him, near the place where he fell, the sulphurous smoke that would have stifled him was rising through a crack in the floor of the cave.

No wonder his friends gave him up for lost, for his escape was marvellous.

Down, down, he went, until he found himself on a sandy floor, with a faint light ahead.

The rush and the shock of his fall half dazed him, and he lay there awhile, wondering if it were not all a dream.

Presently he got upon his feet, and with sore limbs made his way towards the light.

Of a verity it was slow work, for this downward descent would have killed many.

"I'm thankful I'm not dead," Bob muttered. "But where am I ?"

It was a longer journey to the light than he thought it was—a good four hundred yards at least ; but at length he reached it, and found himself nearly at the bottom of the mountain, and within easy view of the sea.

But he dare not emerge into the open air, for a little host of the Bokaris was in sight, dancing, capering, and yelling, in recognition of the outburst of their god, the "speaking mountain."

To Bob this was a disappointment, for he had hoped to be able to go out and search for his late companions. But this was impossible.

Away from the mouth of the cave, down to the Bokaris people, it was open ground.

So he lay in hiding, and was compelled to stop there until darkness set in. His late companions had gone by that time, and he was left a prisoner on the island.

Had he been discovered it would have been the end of his career.

Bob was a brave lad, and he saw that his escape would be a question of time.

But he did not at first dream it would be so long as it turned out.

He soon discovered that the Bokaris people for some reason shunned the spot where he was, and he resolved to abide there as much as possible.

His friends, he knew, must either be dead or gone.

At night he crept out and gathered some wild fruit for food, returning to his hiding-place at dawn.

Again the Bokaris assembled, and he gathered from a few words that arose out of the clamour that the cave in which he was hiding was looked upon as the "mouth" of the mountain.

They simply dare not approach it, lest it should speak *death*.

Bob, not being troubled with such fears, and the activity of the mountain having subsided, he felt sure of a good hiding-place.

And there he had to hide for many days, creeping out at night in search of food, which he readily found.

Of the Bokaris he saw little by night, but by day they were ever near his cave, killing animals and feasting with the prodigality of savages.

What they left Bob found very useful.

Weeks, months passed, and Bob lived on, patiently awaiting for the opportunity which came at last.

One afternoon some of the Bokaris appeared, and just below the base of the mountain, on the shore, he saw a canoe with a sail.

The question was, could he get at it and escape? To do this he must not only get off, but far away, without being seen.

He stole out, and looked anxiously to the right and left.

Nobody in sight. It was like a deserted island.

Then he boldly stepped down to the shore, pushed off the canoe, sprang into it, and set the sail.

Anxiously he looked back, but saw nobody.

What had become of the Bokaris?

He ceased to care when he had got a few miles, and, heading the canoe in the direction of the island of his friends, he fastened the sail.

By-and-bye a dreamy sensation came over him, and, despite his efforts to keep awake, he fell asleep.

The canoe kept an even course, the wind veering but a trifle, so no mishap came about.

When Bob awoke all was darkness about him, and he was riding a long, heavy swell.

The sky was overcast, and low-lying clouds bore evidence of an approaching storm. This was a matter of no little concern to the boy maroon.

At sea in a storm with that frail craft was no joking matter. Bob arose and tried to pierce the darkness about him, but was unable to do so.

He trimmed the sail of the little craft and held it at random dead before the wind. Where it would take him he had no means of knowing.

It might be that he would be blown to sea, far out of the range of the Archipelago. Again, he might be blown on to the shore of another island.

This last would have been a not unwelcome incident, for it would be much safer on land than sea with a storm brewing.

So Bob held the tiller steady, and kept peering ahead with all his might, to catch a glimpse of some welcome coast.

It was no enviable position, and he would much rather it had been daylight instead of pitchy gloom. Suddenly the wind freshened, and waves began to comb over the canoe's bow.

Every moment Bob feared that he would be swamped, but he kept up good courage, and held the canoe steadily on her course.

Thus the night hours passed until after midnight, when, suddenly, a great cry escaped Bob's lips.

Directly ahead in the gloom he saw a strange light.

It was like a beacon at the distance, and in the excitement of the moment he fancied that it was the binnacle lantern of some large ship.

Instantly his heart was in his mouth.

The prospect of being picked up by a ship in those lonely latitudes was almost too joyful a matter for his nerves.

He leaped up, and a hoarse cry escaped his lips.

"Now Heaven give me strength to reach that ship," he prayed, fervently.

He headed the canoe for the distant light, and had the satisfaction of seeing it grow larger, which was an indication that he was nearing it.

But as he kept on, a swift realisation dawned upon him.

"My life!" he gasped. "That is no lantern, but the light of a conflagration. Can it be on land? If not, it is certainly a burning ship."

He strained his gaze eagerly, and vainly tried to make out whether the fire was on land or sea.

An idea for a test suddenly occurred to him.

He stood off with the canoe two points upon a new course.

Then he came up into the wind.

This he did several times.

His purpose was to see if the light changed its position.

If it did not the fire was certainly on land. If it did change position, or floated about, it would be safe to say that it was on the water.

"It is on land," muttered Bob. "I wonder what it can be? Perhaps the watch-fire of some native tribe—perhaps the eruption of a small volcano."

There was no other way but to approach closer to the fire. He set the canoe's course dead for it, and held her before the wind.

Every moment the sea grew heavier, and now it was only when atop of some huge wave that Bob saw the light at all.

Suddenly, too, and to the discomfort of his mind, the light began to fade and die out.

In a very short while not a sign of it could be seen. What did this mean?

If a watch-fire, it had been put out; if a conflagration, it had died out of itself.

Bob groaned aloud.

"Why did it not burn a little longer?" he muttered. "At least, until I could have made the land."

However, the boy adventurer shaped his course as near as possible in the darkness for the spot where the light had been.

The swell was now heavy, and a fog was settling. There was a little moisture in the air, and the sullen swash of white caps warned Bob of the oncoming storm.

Fortunately daylight, though dull and drear, was at hand.

Soon Bob would have been enabled to see if land was ahead of him, had it not been for the fog. But the horizon was too much obscured. He could only guess at this and trust in fate.

It was like groping in the dark, like looking for a needle in a haystack, and a stouter heart than Bob's might have quailed.

But fate was not altogether against the boy maroon.

Presently the canoe shot out of the fog bank into clear atmosphere. Not half a mile, dead ahead, were the cliff-bound shores of a tropical isle.

Bob sprang up in the canoe with a great cry of recognition.

It was the welcome oasis he had sought, the island of the Makolos.

He was overwhelmed with joy.

There were the high cliffs, the headland, and the bay, unmistakably.

But what meant the long column of black smoke rising heavenward?

Long before Bob ran the canoe's bow upon the beach the agonising truth was plain to him.

He sprang out upon the sands, and ran up the bank to the village street, or, rather, where it had been.

An awful wail of horror and despair burst from his lips as he saw that naught but desolation and ruin was upon every hand.

Among the dead bodies scattered about he looked for the forms of his friends.

Great sobs of agony burst from him, for he doubted not but that it was a wholesale massacre, and every resident of the isle had been slaughtered.

But a cloud of smoke hid from him the form of a man walking through the ruins.

A sudden turn and they were face to face. Words cannot depict Bob's sensations as he recognised the other.

It was Bud Danton !

The brush of the most talented artist could scarcely do justice to the tableau thus created by the sudden meeting of Bob Spencer and Bud. Danton.

There had been on board the Pelican a natural antagonism between them. This was now intensified to deadly hatred.

Bob's chest rose and fell, his eyes flashed, and his fingers twitched.

" Bud Danton !" he exclaimed, " we meet again."

The villain's face had at first flushed scarlet, then went white, while a malevolent expression succeeded.

He opened his mouth, and a hiss like that of a venomous reptile came from his throat.

" Bob Spencer !" he gasped. " Where did you come from ? Everybody believed you dead."

" Everybody has made a mistake then," said Bob, coolly. " Kind fate has spared my life for the purpose of revenge."

" Revenge !" Danton replied. " What do you mean ?"

" Why do you ask that ? Gaze about you and see the desolation, the ruin, that your fiendishness has consummated. Where are those so dear to me ? Dead—and by your hand."

Danton laughed mockingly.

"Ha ! ha !" he roared. "Quite tragic, is it not ? And you talk of revenge, eh ? Why, you poor fool, don't you see that you have run yourself into a trap ? This whole island is under my domination now."

Bob quivered with suppressed wrath.

"You are a murderer and a coward, Bud Danton !"

"Spare your compliments."

"At least your life shall be cut short."

Bob felt for his pistol. To his dismay he remembered that he had left it in the canoe.

He was unarmed.

Danton divined this, and with a leap placed himself between the boy and the shore.

"Not so fast, my fine lad," he cried, mockingly. "Who is master of the situation now ?"

For a moment Bob's heart sank within him.

But it revived the next moment, when he saw that the pirate captain had no weapon either, except a dirk-knife. Neither did he seem to have any allies near.

Bob did not fear an even hand-to-hand struggle with the villain.

CHAPTER XXIV.

A HAND-TO-HAND CONFLICT.

FIGHT to the death was what Bob most desired. So after the first tremor of apprehension his manner changed.

"Who is master of the situation is a question to be decided!" he cried, in a ringing voice, as he proceeded to roll up his sleeves.

Danton was astounded.

"What are you going to do?" he asked.

"You shall see. There is a debt between us which only blood can settle, Bud Danton!"

"You mean that?"

"I do."

"And you mean to fight—me?"

"Yes."

"Pshaw! You are a fool."

"We shall see."

"I could break you in two. Don't be rash, boy."

"That is a question to be decided," said Bob, a second time. "I mean to fight you to the death. It is an unequal struggle, for you have a dirk, while I have nothing but my hands."

"And you mean fight?" asked Danton, incredulously.

"Certainly!"

"That settles it," said the pirate chief, with a scornful laugh, as he threw off his jacket.

They were now partly stripped to the waist, and faced each other.

A spectator would at once have noticed the muscular proportions of Danton's frame, but the eye of a physical enthusiast would have dwelt momentarily on them to pass quickly and admiringly to the symmetrical contour of Bob Spencer's shoulders and chest.

Many pounds lighter in frame, the boy, however, possessed that wonderful well-knit, compact build which the gymnast aspires to. In elasticity and durability Bob Spencer's physique, compared with Danton's, was as steel to iron.

Therefore, a judge of physical prowess would not have failed to faithfully foretell the result.

They faced each other, and Bob experienced not the least qualm of fear or doubt.

He was fighting with confidence, with consciousness of right and honour, and also with a purpose.

He was well aware that Danton had comrades not far off.

If these came to his assistance, then his ends would be defeated ; but if not, he would surely triumph.

It was not his purpose to kill Danton, but if possible to make a prisoner of him.

Bob paused a moment, and, gazing penetratingly at his opponent, asked—

"Before we go further, I would like to ask you a question, Bud Danton."

"What is it?"

"Is Phil Farren, my partner, dead ?"

An indescribable light shone in the villain's eyes.

"Yes," he replied.   "He is dead."

But Bob read the lie in his face.

He shrugged his shoulders, drew a breath of relief, and new hope surged into his heart, for he now saw the probable exigency.

The Makolos had been driven from their village, and, with Phil and Mr. Cameron at their head, had retreated into the interior.

As if in confirmation of this surmise a sound now reached Bob's ears.

This was the distant crack of fire-arms.   In an instant his blood was at boiling point.

He longed to fly to the aid of his friends.

" You have lied to me, Bud Danton," he declared, pointedly.   " But I could expect nothing better."

Danton made a sudden spring forward and attempted to close with his foe.   He held the dirk knife in his right hand.

But Bob was too agile.

He evaded the close encounter, and letting out with his right fist gave the villain a stunning blow.

For a moment Danton was blinded.

Bob was not slow to seize the advantage, and rushing in on his foe dashed the knife from his grasp, then, with a dexterous trip of the foot, sent the pirate to the ground.

It was a swift and signal victory.

In an instant Bob was upon him, and dealt him a blow behind the ear which stunned the villain. Before he could recover Bob had removed his jacket, and, knotting it tightly, secured his arms behind him.

Bud Danton was *hors de combat.*

In his victory Bob had been aided not a little by circumstances.

Yet it was an even thing that he would always have defeated Danton in a hand-to-hand encounter.

The vanquished villain fumed and raved, and in vain strove to break his bonds.   This was useless, and he finally saw fit to desist.

He lay upon the ground glaring savagely at his captor.

Bob was now in a quandary what to do.

It was his desire to rejoin his comrades, and still hold Danton as a prisoner. But how he was to do this was a question.

To leave him there for any length of time would be hardly safe.

There was but one way and Bob adopted it

It chanced that there was no time to lose, for suddenly a couple of Bokari warriors appeared through the line of smoke.

To be seen by them would be a fatal thing, and to add to the seriousness of the situation Danton gave a loud yell.

CHAPTER XXV.

OVER THE EDGE.

OB'S heart sank like lead when he saw the Bokari warriors suddenly turn, attracted by Danton's outcry.

Instant action was what the exigency demanded, and Bob did not fail to adopt it. He sprang upon Danton and placed a hand over his mouth.

In an instant he had improvised a gag, and inserted it between his teeth.

This put an end to any further outbreak.

But the mischief had already been done.

The Bokari warriors, having heard the cry, were

not satisfied to let it go uninvestigated. They approached the spot swiftly.

By keeping a crouching position Bob was out of sight, and he at once adopted a clever ruse.

Seizing Danton by the shoulders, he dragged the villain along until the smoke cloud was again between him and the Bokaris.

Then he gave the recumbent villain a sharp kick, and cried—

" Get upon your feet. Make an effort to escape and I will kill you."

Bob held the knife over the pirate captain. He dared not disobey.

In this manner Bob made his prisoner rapidly cross the burned district, until he came to the edge of the forest.

Once under its arches Bob felt safe, as nothing more was seen of the Bokaris.

In the meanwhile a plan of action had suggested itself to the boy.

To attempt to march Danton safely into the Makolo camp, he feared, would not be a possibility.

He bethought himself of the cavern in the cliff where he and Phil had sought refuge on first coming to the island.

" If I put him in there," he muttered, " ascend to the top of the cliff, and draw the ladder after me, he could not escape. There he would be safe."

To conceive the idea was to act upon it.

He at once started for the cavern, marching his foe before him.

Danton was quite docile now, but Bob saw that this was only a feint. His cunning brain was busily at work.

It required some time and climbing to reach the cliff.

Arrived there, the question presented itself as to how he was to get his prisoner into the place.

Bob could hear the distant discharge of guns, and a queer fact presented itself.

He listened intently.

"Strange," he muttered. "There certainly was the discharge of half-a-dozen pieces. Who can be firing. Only Phil and Cameron have firearms."

He was thrilled with astonishment, and somewhat puzzled for a time.

What if some ship's crew were indeed upon the island, and helping the Makolos? He was resolved to join his friends as quickly as possible.

He was not long in hitting upon an idea as to how he was going to get his prisoner into the cave.

Securing Danton's feet with the aid of his own jacket, he left his prisoner helpless upon the cliff, and then descended to the cave.

When he returned he had with him all the rope in the place.

He fastened a long piece of this under Danton's arms.

The villain now began to make signs with his hands as well as he was able.

Bob removed the gag.

"What do you want?" he asked.

"What are you going to do with me?" asked the pirate captain.

"I am going to lower you over the face of the cliff into the cave."

"What then?"

"I shall leave you there until I see fit to call for you."

The villain's face was ashy pale.

"You are not going to let me fall over that cliff?" he asked.

Bob laughed scornfully.

"So that is what you are afraid of, eh?" he asked. "You need not fear. I do not wish to take your worthless life. Retribution will overtake you before long."

"And you mean to leave me in the cave?"

"Yes."

"For how long?"

"Until your miserable allies, the cannibals, have been driven off this island."

Danton's face did not relax its pallor. He could see nothing bright in the outlook.

"Look here, Bob Spencer," he said, in a pleading voice, "I want to talk sense with you."

"My time is limited."

"But I beg of you to listen. You know that I am a man of my word."

"I know nothing of the sort."

"Well, you know I would not break my oath."

"Ugh!" grunted Bob. "I would not care to chance it."

"But I swear to you."

"What?"

"If you will spare my life and set me free I will quit this island and never molest you again. More than that, I will call off the cannibals and leave the Makolo people in peace."

Bob hesitated a moment.

"Do you mean that?"

"I do."

"You will make the Bokari people leave the island?"

"Yes."

"What assurance am I to have that you will do this thing?"

"My word."

The boy shook his head.

"That will not do," he declared.

A baffled light shone in the villain's eyes.

"Then you won't take my word?" he asked.

"Why should I? Have you not proved yourself a rascal, a murderer, and a monster in crime? Am I not justified?"

The crafty villain now simulated deprecation and despair commingled.

"Oh! have mercy," he cried, in distress. "I have no other means of satisfying you. My word is all that I can give. I doubly swear it, that I will leave this island and never trouble you again. Why will you not take my word?"

Bob gazed hard at the villain.

"You dare to ask me that, Bud Danton," he said, in scathing tones. "Look back at my little experience of you. Who was it formed the vile plot against the master of the Pelican, and crept down into the cabin and murdered him in cold blood. Who set us ashore, marooned us upon a desolate isle, with the belief that we would die? Was it not you? Think you that a man base enough to do all this will scruple to break his word? Never will I trust you!"

Danton did not speak again, but his eyes gleamed with a devilish light.

There was naught but murder in his heart then.

Bob wasted no more time in discussion, but took a turn with the rope, now tied under Danton's arms, around a large boulder

Then he lowered his tightly bound captive until

he was on a level with the mouth of the cliff cave. Bob now descended the rope ladder, and it was an easy matter to swing his prisoner in upon the cavern floor.

This feat accomplished, Bob untied the rope, and winding it up, prepared to return to the top of the cliff.

CHAPTER XXVI.

WALLED IN.

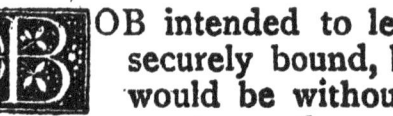OB intended to leave Danton in the cave securely bound, but even were he free he would be without means of ascent or descent over the smooth walls of the cliff.

But at this juncture Fortune's wheel made an unlucky turn for the boy.

While winding up the rope he stood with his back to the prostrate villain.

Like a flash, Danton, who had in some inexplicable manner freed his bonds, sprung up, and with a hoarse yell precipitated his weight against Bob.

As a stone from a catapult Bob Spencer shot out of the cavern mouth, and went down through the air to a seemingly horrible death.

.   .   .   .

Led on by their chief, the Bokaris were coming up the gorge in overwhelming numbers.

With the reinforcements which they had received they anticipated little trouble in sweeping the balance of the Makolo tribe from the face of the earth.

Therefore the reception which they met with was a genuine surprise to them.

Cameron and Phil, at the right and left of the

Makolo line, held their men well in hand until the foe were quite near.

Then the order rang out—

"Ready! Fire!"

The next instant a deafening volley of musketry rent the air of the gorge.

Most of the Makolos fired at random.

Some did not fire at all, having pressed the guard instead of the trigger, or from other causes.

Some of the bullets of course went high, but the volley on the whole was destructive, sweeping the Bokaris down like wheat before the reaper.

The effect was tremendous.

The cannibals, probably inferring from the number of guns that there were more than two white men in the party, became panic-stricken.

Once more the Makolos poured a volley into their ranks.

This was sufficient.

With terror they broke and incontinently fled. Down the gorge they went in wild confusion.

Matafayo and his men were wildly jubilant, and were for making a sally and annihilating the foe.

But the cooler leaders, Phil and Mr. Cameron, restrained them.

"For the present we must maintain the defensive," Mr. Cameron declared.

Bud Danton was not present to rally the Bokaris, so they retreated until once more in the valley.

Here, finding that they were not pursued, they halted and began to reform.

The first panic over, their courage in a measure returned.

It could not be said of the Bokaris that they were cowards.

A conference was held between the chiefs, when it was not deemed expedient to battle on even ground with bows and arrows against the deadly fire-sticks. How there came to be so many of them in the gorge was a great mystery.

The Bokaris suspected a trick. The two white men must have shifted their position very rapidly with their two fire-sticks.

It was not dreamed of as a fact that the Makolos were all armed with the deadly fire-sticks.

After much palaver it was decided to make a second attack in a different direction, and this time not to waver until their line was over the enemy's breastworks.

The cannibals once more returned to the assault, filling the gorge like a pestilential swarm of flies.

On they went until scarcely fifty yards were between them and the enemy's position.

Suddenly there rose into view fully two hundred of the Makolos with fire-sticks, so called, at their shoulders.

Once more the roar of small arms filled the gorge, and once more the Bokari line wavered.

But this time they were to keep on to the top, and they still struggled forward.

Once more the Makolos poured a tremendous volley into their ranks.

It caused a frightful loss of life, and the Bokaris began to waver.

They fired volley after volley of arrows, which had no effect upon the enemy, concealed as they were behind the stone breastworks.

As fast as the carbines were fired, Mr. Cameron had another line of men in the rear reloading, so that a continuous fire was kept up.

As one line of men stepped down another stepped up ready to fire.

There could have been but one ending to the affair had the Bokaris persisted in the attack—which was their utter annihilation.

But they had sufficient good sense to break ranks and retreat after the third volley.

Fully one-fifth of their number lay dead in the gorge.

It was a signal victory for the Makolos, and they rent the air with their loud cries.

The Bokaris, discomfited, retired to the plain below. They did not return to the attack.

The Makolos now had a breathing spell, and they improved the opportunity.

Mr. Cameron, who was overjoyed with the result, wrung Phil's hand in an enthusiastic manner.

"We shall teach those monsters a lesson," he declared, exultantly. "They will never attack our people again. I tell you, Phil, we will yet make warriors of these people."

"I am afraid our dreams of empire will miscarry," Phil declared, solemnly. "Our projected city is in ashes."

"But we can rebuild."

"I fear not."

"Why?"

A great change had taken place in Phil's ideas. This was occasioned by a very peculiar discovery.

In the excitement of the attack it had been unnoticed by any but himself.

"Come with me," he said, significantly.

Mr. Cameron complied wonderingly, and followed Phil into the cave. When they had penetrated it some distance the youth halted, and said—

"Now, listen, Mr. Cameron, and tell me if you hear anything strange."

The island exile immediately complied.

At first he heard nothing, but very soon there came to his ears a strange, rumbling sound, like distant muffled thunder. Then there was a slight perceptible tremor of the earth.

Mr. Cameron now understood Phil's meaning well enough. He turned deadly pale.

"You hear it?" asked Phil.

"Yes."

"Well, my theory is just this. We know that the island is of volcanic origin. What more natural than that it should at some time be destroyed as swiftly and suddenly as it was made."

"In other words, you do not consider it stable ground?"

"Exactly."

"But is there immediate danger?"

"This strange rumbling sound must indicate a disturbance of some sort in the bowels of the earth. I should say that an eruption of the volcano is apt to take place at any time."

"If it proves nothing worse than that then we have little to fear."

"It all depends upon what sort of an eruption we get."

"Well," said Mr. Cameron, with more confidence, "I think we need not fear much from that source, for we have had several eruptions since I have been on the island, and also a slight earthquake."

"But," said Phil, dubiously, "I have a particular horror of things of the sort. For instance, suppose we built a magnificent city of stone here. At any moment an earthquake might level it to the ground."

"Of course."

"Then this is not the part of the world for progressive men to stake their fortunes."

"I agree with you there," declared Mr. Cameron, readily. "In fact, I think our best plan is to relinquish our golden dreams and take the first opportunity to get back home again."

"I am with you !" cried Phil.

But the words had scarcely left his lips when a terrible thing happened. A mighty rumble, like Heaven's artillery let loose, broke on their ears, and the earth began to heave and toss like the sea.

Both were prostrated, and the air became black as night. When, after some time, Phil was enabled to regain his feet and light a match, a most horrible discovery awaited him.

The cavern-mouth had become blocked. Upon all sides there was naught but impassable rock. They were virtually walled in !

CHAPTER XXIX.
IN THE VILLAIN'S POWER.

OB SPENCER had no chance to save himself, so quick was Danton's onslaught, and he went over the edge like a cannon-ball.

Danton had, with the most strenuous of efforts, succeeded in wrenching one wrist free.

It was then an easy matter for him, with Bob's back turned, to free himself. It was a most remarkable turning of the tables.

But Bob had not gone to his death.

He was saved in a miraculous manner.

The truth being, the tide, which ran high on the sandy beach, was in, and there were full twenty feet of water in the chasm below.

Down into the water Bob went like a rocket.

He happened to strike it right, feet first, and went to the bottom, but quickly came to the surface again. He was unhurt.

His first impulse was to swim to a rock near, and, crawling out of the water, look up.

He saw Danton scaling the rope-ladder and making good his escape.

It galled Bob to witness this.

"All right," he muttered. "We'll see. My time will come yet."

Danton soon reached the top of the cliff, and without an instant's delay set out for the scene of battle.

The villain was triumphant in the belief that he had visited summary vengeance upon one of his foes.

Rejoicing in this conviction, he went on his way rapidly.

He heard the sounds of battle as he ran, and also the crack of musketry, which puzzled him.

"The fiends take it!" he said. "Can it be that some ship's crew has struck the island and is helping them? But it will not save them. I have sworn vengeance, and to have that girl, and have her I will."

He went on with all speed, and at length came upon the scene of the conflict.

He was in time to see his allies, the Bokaris, driven back by the Makolos, who, with their superior weapons, easily held the mastery.

Danton was infuriated when he perceived this state of affairs, and threw himself among the cannibal crew, inciting them by every means in his power to return to the attack.

He succeeded in rallying a few of them, and these had begun a charge upon the enemy's position when the earthquake came.

There was a terrific shaking and trembling of the earth, huge yawning chasms were rent in the solid rock, the sea came in a tidal wave over the lower part of the island, and fearful terror reigned.

The cannibals were effectually routed, and fled, shrieking with terror, to the valleys below—anywhere, everywhere, scarcely knowing whither, while the dread forces of nature were at work.

Even Danton himself, with all his reckless courage, was affrighted.

He crouched upon the ground in terror while the fearful commotion lasted. It was soon over.

But its effects were visible upon every hand.

The whole face of the island had materially changed.

Where there had been hills there were now plains and *vice versa*.

Lakes and streams had changed their courses, and things too wonderful for description had been evolved in the chaos.

The general panic had not been confined to the Bokaris.

The Makolos had also been scattered, and were entirely disbanded.

There was no thought of strife then, and friend and foe alike sought his personal safety.

We have seen the fate of Mr. Cameron and Phil in the cave.

Mida had been in the outer cavern when the shock came.

She had no distinct after-recollection of what happened in that period of time.

It was all a jumbled mass of incidents until she found herself in a lonely glade between high hills, and in a locality with which she was unfamiliar.

The truth was, heavy masses of rock had been falling all about her, and the common impulse had seized her to flee.

She had ran and stumbled on at random until the subsiding of the earthquake had found her in this strange locality.

She was weak and exhausted, and sank down, unable to go further.

After awhile, however, she recovered her strength and powers of recollection.

Then a deep cry of despair welled up from her throat

"Oh, Heaven!" she cried, in agonised accents, "I fear my father and Phil are killed. They, were in the cave, and it must have fallen in upon them."

She almost fainted with the shock of the realisation—then her courage asserted itself. She steeled her nerves, and with white, set lips, and a resolute light in her eyes, said—

"But I must be strong. Perhaps I can save them. Heaven give me strength now!"

With a wonderful calmness she located the position of the cave as well as she could, and started for it. .

She had crossed the glade, and was about to enter a thicket of palms, when a terrified cry escaped her, and she recoiled.

"Ah! my beauty, Fate has served me this turn. Nay, do not flutter so, my pretty bird. I'll not harm you."

From the thicket a man had sprang forth. He was dark and evil-looking, and Mida recognised him at once as her foe—her most dreaded enemy.

It was Bud Danton!

There was a light of devilish triumph in the villain's eyes, and he regarded the young girl with that gloating with which the deadly serpent regards its helpless prey.

Mida could not speak, could not act, so great was her terror.

Bud Danton folded his arms, and gazed at her with a mocking smile and imperturbable ease.

"You see, my lady," he said, in an oily voice,

"that what I told you at our first meeting is certain to become true. Fate has willed it—you are sure to be mine."

Mida drew back with all the scorn and loathing she felt. She had found her voice, and replied—

"I regard it as unfortunate that I should meet so great a villain as you alone. Yet I have no fear. You can do me no harm."

Danton affected tenderness.

"Really, my dear," he simpered, "I would not harm you for the world. You will find that I have a heart which is moved by the dictates of compassion and honour."

Mida was quick to turn the point to her advantage.

"You speak of honour," she said, scathingly. "If you have such an element in your composition you will stand aside and allow me to pass."

"Then you would leave me?"

"I have no business with you."

"I cannot permit any sense of honour to interfere with the promptings of love," said the villain.

"Which proves that you are not a gentleman, who holds chivalry and honour before everything."

"I adhere to practicality, not to poesy," replied Danton, ungallantly. "It is a question of vital importance to me. Shall I sacrifice my life's joy and allow the beautiful prize to slip from me, when, by a bold, desperate stroke, I may win it? All that I have ever gained, *ma chère*, has been gained in that manner."

With a wild laugh Danton cast aside the vari-coloured sash which enveloped his shoulders, and, with a quick bound, threw his arm about Mida's slender waist.

"You are mine or all time," he cried. "Nothing can wrest you from me, my peerless prize. Not all the powers of Heaven and earth. I swear it !"

CHAPTER XXX.

A LUCKY ESCAPE.

MORE fearful situation could hardly be conceived than that in which Phil Farren and Mr. Cameron found themselves.

Moreover, the earthquake was not yet over, and kept up a rocking motion which was most frightful to experience.

Walled in with rock !

How deep it was, or how the barrier could ever be overcome or penetrated, were agonising questions to both.

It seemed an age before the force of the earthquake subsided.

At length, however, the dreadful tossing and trembling of the ground abated, and they were enabled to take a calmer survey of their situation.

This brought no encouraging ideas, though.

Mr. Cameron and Phil went about in the dark, groping for some sort of an outlet to their prison cell.

They were hemmed in on all sides, as it seemed, by massive walls of rock.

There was no likelihood that anybody would endeavour to reach them from the outside, for they would hardly guess their position.

It was a moment of blank, awful despair.

"Heaven help us, Phil!" exclaimed Mr. Cameron, in shaking tones. "I believe that we are surely lost."

Phil could not speak for some moments. The bare realisation seemed to appall him.

"We are doomed to die in this horrible place," he gasped, finally.

"There is no help for us."

"It would take a steam-drill weeks to cut us out of here."

"The end has come."

So it indeed seemed.

The conviction was so strong that both were overwhelmed. But in a measure resignation soon came to relieve Phil's suffering of mind.

"What will become of Mida?" groaned Mr. Cameron. "I don't care for myself, but for my darling child."

"You can only commend her to the care of an ever-watchful Providence," said Phil. "We cannot help her now."

Mr. Cameron groaned aloud. But Phil advanced and took one of his hands.

"Don't forget," he said, impressively, "that we are men, and should meet death with fortitude. It is the common lot of mankind."

"I care not for myself," repeated the island exile, "but for my child. Alas! how have all our golden dreams miscarried."

"Yes—dispelled in an hour," agreed Phil. "If we were even now out of this I should give up the plan of founding a city on this isle. It would not endure. These earthquakes are probably of great frequency."

"You are right," agreed Mr. Cameron. "Oh! for a look at dear old England once more."

"Aye!" cried Phil, "to be back once more in my happy boyhood home. I would never leave it."

"You are sensible. A roving, adventurous life don't pay. After all, earthly happiness is found only in the sum total of home."

"If I could only get home I would stay there."

Thus the two imprisoned adventurers bemoaned their fate.

But it is said truly that hope dies last of all, and it was not long before Phil began to again search the cavern.

This time he was cooler, and went to work more systematically.

The result was that he chanced to discover in the blackness overhead a little ray of light.

"Hurrah!" he cried. "We have looked everywhere but up there, Mr. Cameron. Perhaps we may find an outlet to the cave even now."

In an instant Mr. Cameron was alive with new hope and courage.

By reaching out they ascertained that they could not touch the cavern roof.

But Phil presently found that he could climb upwards by means of jagged, projecting rocks.

With Mr. Cameron's assistance he climbed up them, and soon had got sufficiently close to the aperture to see that it was large enough to admit his hand.

He looked up into daylight, and saw stars in the blue sky.

He placed a hand against the ledge of rock above and pushed it.

To his amazement it moved, and he saw that the aperture was enlarged. A cry of joy escaped his lips.

Again he pushed it, and again it moved. The opening was now a foot in breadth, and with re-doubled exertions Phil had soon increased the aper-ture to three feet.

It was now large enough for him to climb up through, which he did, and stood in the open air—free from the imprisonment which had seemed, a short while before, certain death.

Mr. Cameron followed him quickly, and they clasped hands as they stood once more under the glorious light of mid-day.

It seemed like a miracle, and each at that moment instinctively murmured prayers of thanks to the Power whose sway is supreme. Then they looked about them.

CHAPTER XXIX.

FINIS.

PHIL and Mr. Cameron were on the crest of a hill, a sort of rocky ledge, and a good view of the valley below could be had.

Not a sign of the natives anywhere could be seen. Indeed, not another living being was in sight.

"Great Heavens!" gasped Mr. Cameron, "they cannot have been all destroyed. Where have they gone, Phil?"

Phil was unable to reply.

For some moments they stood irresolute; then a sudden recollection came to Mr. Cameron.

"I must find Mida," he cried. "Oh! I fear harm has come to her."

They descended to the mouth of the cavern, which was now hermetically sealed with ledges of rock.

Not a trace of the Makolos could be found.

It was evident that they had incontinently fled, their superstitious terror of the earthquake impelling them.

Of course Mida was not found, and Mr. Cameron was in doubt as to her fate.

He did not waste time in deliberation, but quickly took the only course left him, and began a search.

In this he was guided by a strange prescience. It impelled him toward the coast.

Of course Phil accompanied him, and they went on rapidly in their quest. But search as they would, not a trace of the missing young girl could be found.

Mr. Cameron was frantic with despair when they came suddenly out upon a cliff which looked seaward.

The long, unbroken horizon line was spread before them.

The sea was a beautiful amber and gold tint in the declining rays of the sun.

Both stood gazing at the lovely spectacle, when suddenly a wild, startled cry broke from the lips of each.

Around a headland, her taper masts being first visible, swung the trim hull of a first-class merchant ship.

At her peak floated the English flag.

It was like an apparition to the two island castaways. For a moment it seemed as if they were dreaming, and the ship was all a strange unreality.

"A ship!" gasped Mr. Cameron. "As I live, Phil Farren, it is an English brig."

Phil Farren's heart almost stood still. At that moment it appeared as if he could not bear the strain of the great joy forced upon him.

Then a wild, passionate cry burst from his lips, and he swung his arms over his head in unrestrained glee.

"A ship—a ship! We are saved," he cried, excitedly. "Saved! Thank Heaven, we are saved!"

Down to the sandy beach below the two exiles ran madly.

They saw that they were observed by those on board the vessel, and heard the mighty splash and the ringing of the chain as the heavy anchor went thundering and boiling down into the water of the bay.

Then a hail was heard.

"Ahoy! the island."

"Ahoy! the ship," replied Phil.

"Who are you?"

" We are castaways from the wrecked ship, Pelican. I will tell you all if you will take us off."

" Stand by, and we will send a boat."

In a few moments a cutter was clipping the wave crests of the bay, and Phil and Mr. Cameron entering it were rowed back to the ship.

The name upon her hull was—" Mary Robinson !"

Bob Spencer reclimbed the cliff he had been pushed off of as rapidly as possible, but not in time to get a sight of Danton again.

The villain had given him the slip, and was ere this well in the interior of the isle.

Nevertheless, Bob endeavoured to track him, and was engaged in this pursuit when the earthquake took place.

For a time Bob fancied that the end of the world had come, and it was some while before he recovered from the effects of a severe shaking up.

Fortunately, however, he was not seriously injured. After the affair was past, he had hardly time to collect his scattered senses when another thrilling incident occurred. Suddenly from the copse a lot of natives, wild with terror, burst and ran past him like maniacs. They were the Bokaris fleeing to the valley below.

In their flight they passed Bob so closely that he might have touched them.

On they went madly.

Bob guessed the reason of their frenzy, though he could not help watching them with wonderment. But this state of affairs did not last long.

Bob knew that their panic would terminate with the earthquake, and then his position would be one fraught with danger.

To again fall into the power of the Bokaris would mean certain death.

Therefore he resolved to change his position, and he started to skirt the valley, in the hope of falling in with the Makolos.

But he had not covered a half mile when, emerging into a small glade, he came face to face with three Bokari warriors.

They instantly recognised him, and as they had now recovered from their panic, they did not hesitate to attack him.

It was plain to Bob that they meant to take his life.

His face paled.

It was heavy odds—three against one—but he never lost courage. He drew forth a pistol he had found in the cave, and with the only cartridge left in it shot one of the brutes dead.

The other two, brandishing their javelins, descended upon him.

One of the keen weapons grazed Bob's shoulder. The other he grasped before the Bokari warrior could throw it.

Then he grappled with his foes.

The Bokari warriors were both now unarmed, and it became a question of physical superiority.

So far as brute strength went there was no doubt that Bob was over matched.

But the boy hero was an adept wrestler. The moment that the shiny black bodies of the cannibal warriors closed upon him he seized one by a queer sort of back hitch, and flung him upon his head with such force that he was momentarily stunned.

This gave him time to cope with the other. It was a quick, sharp tussle.

The Bokari seemed confident of winning ; but while he had superior strength he had not the skill.

Bob wrestled with him easily a moment ; then he made a feint of seizing him by the shoulders, and, clutching him by the thighs, swung him to the left and underneath.

Then he grasped the javelin which lay near and drove it into his foe's breast. It was a death stroke.

Meanwhile the third Bokari had regained his feet, but he incontinently fled. He did not care to dispute the way with so valorous an antagonist.

Bob was left the victor, and he had conquered with hardly loss of breath. He stood for a moment undecided what move next to make when he heard footsteps.

Instantly he sank out of sight in some bushes, and waited for the unknown to appear, which he did in a moment, passing so near that Bob could have sprung upon him.

But the boy was electrified as he recognised the new comer. It was Bud Danton.

Danton was creeping stealthily along, evidently upon the watch for somebody. Bob held his breath as he now saw the cause for this move upon the villain's part.

Into the glade a slender form had glided. It was Mida Cameron.

And there, secreted in the copse, Bob had watched the meeting between the two, and did not stir until he saw Danton throw his arms about Mida.

Then all the chivalry of his nature was aroused. Like a young lion he sprang upon the villain.

Danton was completely taken aback at the sudden

attack on his rear, and, as he turned to face Bob Spencer, for a moment he was appalled with cowardly fear.

"Scoundrel!" cried Bob with righteous indignation, "you shall not carry out your villainous intentions. Your devilish career is near its end."

"Say you so!" said the villain, regaining courage as he saw that Bob was alone. "You will find that Bud Danton never knows defeat. Take that!"

He aimed a blow at Bob, but the youth had the javelin poised, and thrust it into the villain's shoulder.

With a cry of pain Danton dropped his arm, and before he could make resistance again, Bob had thrown him violently and was binding his arms and ankles with a species of vine growing near.

In a few moments he was helpless, and a prisoner.

Then Mida came up to Bob and took his arm. Tears streamed from her eyes as she thanked her brave rescuer.

It did not take Bob long to decide upon a plan of action.

He concluded that, as the isle was overrun with cannibals, it would be safer to seek refuge in the cliff-house.

So, leaving Danton until some future convenient occasion served to remove him from the spot, Bob took Mida's arm and set out for the cliff-house.

It was not long before they reached the sandy shore, and they had just turned an angle in the cliff when a wild cry of joy rose upon the air.

The next moment Mr. Cameron had his beloved Mida in his arms, and Phil was embracing Bob with a transport of joy.

They had just come ashore from the Mary Robinson, and the meeting was opportune.

Pen cannot describe it.

"Dear old friend!" cried Phil, frantically, "I thought you went to your death on the Bokari Isle."

Right then and there mutual confidences were exchanged, explanations made, and then all went aboard the Mary Robinson.

It was a happy ending of a long series of thrilling and terrible experiences.

* * * * * * *

A delegation from the ship's crew accompanied Bob to take Danton off the isle.

But they might have spared themselves the trouble.

A horrible fate had befallen the villain.

In Bob's absence a man-eating tiger happened to come along, and the wretch was torn limb from limb. It was an awful expiation of a life of crime.

Of course, the idea of civilising the Makolos and colonising the island was abandoned, and preparations were made for leaving.

But the captain of the Mary Robinson kindly sent armed men ashore and drove the Bokaris from the isle with great slaughter, reinstating the Makolos.

Captain Black's treasure was brought off and divided, making a snug little fortune for all.

It was just six months later when Phil Farren set foot in his native land again.

Accompanied by Bob, he went straight to his uncle's house, where, to his great joy, he was received with quite an ovation.

He learned what he little hoped for, that the stain

of crime had long been removed from his shoulders, and the next morning he visited the old school.

There he had a reception he is not likely to forget, nor the boys either.

He was allowed to give a school treat, and such an evening had never been spent there before or since.

Mr. Cameron and Mida went north and settled down; but they correspond with Phil, who now and then runs up to see them.

People say that something is likely to come of these visits by-and-bye, and, no doubt, they are right.

Neither Bob or Phil, though fairly well to do, live an idle life.

They have taken to farming together, and, considering the times, they do very well.

May good fortune continue to dwell with the two plucky boys.

THE END.